A RAVING MONARCHIST

JULIAN RATHBONE

A Raving Monarchist

ST. MARTIN'S PRESS

NEW YORK

Library of Congress Cataloging in Publication Data
Rathbone, Julian, 1935–
    A raving monarchist.

    I. Title.
PZ4.R232Rav   1978   [PR6068.A8]   823'.9'14
ISBN 0-312-66412-5   77-9127

This book is for my Mother
There is little in it
that will offend her and, I hope,
much that will entertain

Contents

NOTE

Juan Carlos I, King of Spain, and Santiago Martín (also known as *Su Majestad*) are not my creations – the media in Spain and elsewhere must take the credit. I have praised one to the skies and I hold the other in deepest respect. I hope neither will mind their brief appearances in these pages, doing things on particular days in 1976 that, by and large, they actually did.

The rest, all the rest, is fiction.

PROLOGUE

It seems I have to wait at least a week to learn if Maurice will ever walk again, if his brain is severely damaged, if indeed he will live.

I must try not to be too hopeful: an hour or so ago they wheeled him out of the operating theatre and back to the intensive care unit. In spite of the brightness of new dressings, the smooth perfection of the turned down sheet, the gleam of chrome and glass on all the appliances strapped to him and slotted into him, he looks a mess. Eight hours after his fall, bruising is already swelling dark purple round his eyes and mouth, several of the minor lacerations have been left uncovered—stitched with black thread in places and all daubed with vermilion mercurichrome, his legs are in plaster and under traction. He is still in what appears to be a deep coma. The surgeon, whose English is exemplary, said that it may be some days before he recovers full consciousness: if he ever does.

The police have found me a hotel room – in the Hostal de España, Rúa del Villar – a very considerable achievement here in Santiago de Compostela on St James's Day, in a Holy Year. Someone must have been kicked out. There are advantages in being in a police state, especially when you have just done the state some service. It's a comfortable place – rather old-fashioned with tiled floors, a private lav called the Niagara made in Stoke-on-Trent, and solid furniture with shiny brass fittings. Maurice would have loved it. There's a big double bed too. The only drawback is the noise outside – a constant babble of voices from the street (fortunately closed to traffic), distant cheers, fire-crackers, music . . .

. . . I've just looked out of the window. A Galician pipe-band, kilted, squawling, yet oddly un-Scottish, was swinging by. I hope things quieten down at night. But I don't suppose they will.

I started writing this ten minutes ago. It now occurs to me that I should go on – or rather go back. Go back to

13

the beginning and record the whole business. I don't suppose anyone will read it if Maurice dies, but it will give me something to do while I wait. Yes. And there have been good things too, as well as the awful ones, and it would be good to write it all up while the memories are still clear . . .

. . . I have just come back from the lounge. The manager called me down, insisted that I watch the ceremonies in the Cathedral on his colour television. They were impressive, gorgeous. The King read his message to the Nation, or his Rededication of the Nation to St James, or something of the sort. He looked a most impressive figure, and certainly I received a clearer view of him than I got last night when I saw him in the flesh. Tall, with short bronze wavy hair, he carries himself well, with easy dignity. He has the air of one on whom the cares of state already weigh heavily but you feel they are a burden he can cope with. It's noticeable how much royalty there is in his face – Bourbon, Saxe-Coburg, even Hapsburg, it's all there. I wonder, is there a drop of Spanish blood at all? It's odd to think that after forty-three years of Republicanism and then Franco, he's come back, the grandson of the last king, with more power in his hands than any other sovereign in Europe, as much power constitutionally I believe as the President of France.

When it was finished and the processions were moving back down the noble wide nave, I turned to the manager, who has a little English, and asked him what the King had said.

'Very much religious. Not much important. But he says he seeks a reign of Justice; he will have care for and embrace Peace, Reconciliation, a noble living together in Liberty with Order and Tolerance, based on Mutual Respect, and so on, and so on.'

'Does he mean it?' I asked.

'He means it,' the little hotelier replied. Then added with a shrug, 'It remains that he must be allowed.'

14

The picture switched to the huge square outside the Cathedral, packed solid with thirty, forty thousand people: 'Juan Car-los, Juan Car-los, Juan Car-los,' they chanted.

I came back upstairs to think about Maurice, and get on with this account of how we came to be here – I in a hotel room; he plastered from toes to pelvis and plugged into the intensive care unit in the hospital in Santiago de Compostela, the Shrine of Spain, on Sant'Iago's Day, 25th July 1976.

I'm very tired though. I have not slept for thirty-six hours. Perhaps I should try to rest a little first.

PART ONE

The Pyrenees

CHAPTER 1

'I can't say I find them wildly attractive.'

The two lines of dancers, all children, both sexes, ages five to fifteen, capered in front of each other shifting the semi-circular hoops they held above their heads from side to side. The hoops were garlanded with red and green paper which the gusty wind threatened to shred.

'Interesting though,' I replied; then, aware that Maurice had raised his left eyebrow in an expression of quizzical disdain, I qualified lamely: 'I suppose.'

'Ethnically?' he spaced out the syllables. 'Anthropologically?'

The two columns were now threading their way through an arch of hoops which grew into a tunnel as each new pair got through. I thought of offering a comment on the survival of labyrinthine patterns in folk dance, but resisted.

'Hardly,' I said.

The dance came to an end; the large crowd, driven off the beaches by the squally weather, applauded heartily and two of the older children took the hoops off the others. The bossy adult in charge issued pieces of thick dowelling two feet long, two to each boy. The flutes struck up a smarter rhythm, the drums rattled militantly.

'Politically,' I suggested. 'I mean, I suppose they are Basques.'

The boys now formed into fours and began to clatter the heavy batons together, rather like the clap-hand games children play in England, but more complicated. They were dressed in black berets, grey smocks, black breeches and, like the girls, wore slippers that were kept on by thongs cross-laced up over their shins.

19

'Oh yes. They're Basques. Indeed they are.'

Maurice shivered, turned up the collar of his wash-leather fringed jacket, first shaking his head so his long, very black shiny hair fell inside it. 'I suppose this would be quite a good moment for some terrorist to let off a bomb,' he added.

The square was densely packed around the space where the troupe was performing. Looking out over the heads of the crowd – we were on the edge of it, on the steps leading up to the portico of the church – the mind rejected the horror of a sudden explosion.

'Rather counter-productive I should have thought. I mean what would be the point of a terrorist blowing up a whole lot of his own people?'

'The terrorism is by no means one-sided.' Again his tone was faintly snubbing. 'In fact it's arguable the other side started it. Anyway I'm bored.' He slipped his hand through my arm, quite without shyness, in a way which still made my heart skip a little and which I had missed during nine months' separation, and steered me away from the crowd towards the stone balustrade and tossing tamarisks beyond.

In a moment or two the wind and the surf obliterated the mewling of the flutes. Below us the rollers surged in off the Atlantic, with streamers of foam along their crests, to crash against the brown cliffy headland sending plumes almost to the step of the lighthouse; or right on up the cove they came before breaking only yards short of the squat ugly casino at the sea's edge. Low cloud raced in above them and between it and the surf a solitary gull rode on the wind for a moment before tipping its wings to be carried inshore over palms and mimosas, hotels and stores and blocks of luxury flats. It was 28th of June, Biarritz, the weather was horrible, and I had left an England already in the grip of the drought.

We followed the neat walk that zig-zagged round and down the headland towards the crowded pools of what had once been a fishing harbour. Expensive yachts bobbed and swayed, rigging and tackle clacked percussively.

'It must have been a lousy crossing. Are you very exhausted?' Maurice murmured solicitously.

I had driven off the car ferry at San Sebastián that morning.

'It wasn't too bad really. The sea didn't get up until late yesterday evening. And I'm a good sailor.'

'Of course you are.' His face lit up with affection. 'I think you're a lovely sailor.' He squeezed my hand and went on: 'No, actually the weather here didn't break till last night. The most wonderful thunderstorm and the first rain of the whole month. Where shall we go? You'd like a drink before we leave? There's not much point in hanging around on a day like this.'

A few minutes later we were in Les Colonnes, very comfortably placed in soft leather chairs. Around us a hundred old ladies, all beautifully groomed and coiffured, sipped lemon tea (*le five o'clock*), and the light, already reflected and refracted by mirrors and cut glass, flashed from their rings.

'I can't really believe there's much in the way of terrorism here. It's too like Bournemouth to be true.'

'Isn't it just?' And there shone the eager smile I remembered so well. 'Bournemouth before the lumpen proletariat discovered it. The shops sell Real Old Harrogate Toffee, there's a Lloyds Bank, and the bookshop is called The Book Shop. No, all the terrorism is over the border,' he went on, 'in Spain. Mind, there have been one or two explosions, and one or two shootings. But all very personal, I think. Rival groups of refugees bumping each other off, and one house got bombed: apparently it had been rented by Los Guerilleros de Cristo Rey. Are you paying? Then I'll have a large Suze.'

'Who are they?'

'Oh you know.' Slightly impatient. 'Warriors of Christ the King. Far Right. *Ultras*. All absolutely nasty,

21

all absolutely mad. Five of them bought a house here as a base for spying on Spanish Basques who operate from around here, but the Basques blew them up.'

I sipped my Stella Artois and looked across at him. He was paler, thinner than he had been, and the whites of his large eyes were a little jaundiced. He fiddled with his glass, swishing the ice cubes round in it and I noticed dirt in his finger nails. There was a stain on his very expensive jacket – I knew just how expensive, I had bought it for him as a going-away present. I felt a little spasm of longing, of tenderness, something almost paternal perhaps. Well, he'll get over whatever he's been up to now, I thought; six weeks motoring round Spain with no worries and only the most harmless sort of vice ought to pull him round. I smiled at him and, caught by surprise, he grinned back, then his eyes sheered off again.

'Bloody Basques,' he said. 'They get on my tits.'

During the hour it took to steer my converted Transit van through the traffic that had congealed between Biarritz and Bayonne, Maurice laconically quizzed me about what had been happening at the university. He wasn't that interested. I don't think he was ever really interested in people unless they were under his nose; however, he had a giggle or two over the latest news on his moral tutor.

Dr Stukely had been gay, maybe would be again one day, but had recently married a jolly plump girl who had hung his walls with jolly wallpaper and filled his house with plump furniture. To finish it off, she was now even plumper and due to bifurcate in the autumn. Stukely in his gay days had introduced me to Maurice and when Pam began to loom had not been too bitchy about letting me take over where he had left off. He is a lecturer in Spanish, was Maurice's moral tutor; Maurice is a student of French and Spanish; I lecture in English at the same university. Maurice had just finished his compulsory nine months in France as an *assistant* in the Lycée at Pau and was about to embark on a compulsory three months in Spain—partly at the state's expense, but mostly at mine.

It was the end of June. I had come out to pick him up, via San Sebastián to avoid a boring drive through the duller side of France, and he had arranged to meet me at Biarritz. In London the lions in the zoo were ill with heat, the M.C.C. was ill with West Indians, and all the way from Bayonne to Pau it poured relentlessly, torrentially.

CHAPTER 2

'It was like this from November to April,' Maurice said as I peered through the segment of clear glass the wipers sliced out of the sheets of water that were now sliding down the windscreen. Vision came and went in strobo-scopic rhythm and I wondered aloud if I should pull in until it eased up.

'Oh I doubt if it will. Not for days. September was dry, May was only moist, June has been lovely up to now. Now we're back to normal. And watch out for the other drivers,' he added as a Peugeot thundered by send-ing up a bow wave that broke along the side of the van, 'they are mad, mad, mad.'

'I've already noticed.'

'I can go on about the rain at some length. You've no idea how deadening it was to turn up day after day at the Lycée, soaked to the skin, to be asked inevitably every day, "Did I not feel at home? It must be just like Eng-land." '

And then a little later: 'We are now in Béarn. We have left the Pays Basque. The French have a saying, I expect you know it, *il pleut comme une vache qui pisse*. The Béarn coat of arms has *two* cows on it.'

'Apart from the weather what sort of year have you had?' Maurice does not write letters.

'Oh not bad really. Well, most of it. It was a bit mizz at first, but got better. Actually I got off to a bad start. Almost straight away I found a smart little studio flat – modern, all mod cons, fridge, bath, shower, con-stant hot water, all self-contained and quite prettily fur-nished. What silly me had not realised was that it was on the *poids lourds* route: you know, every French town has

24

one, the compulsory way round for heavy lorries. *That* sort of thing.'

We were passing the three largest lorries I have ever seen – they must each have been twenty yards long – parked in a layby.

'I was on the third floor, they thundered by every night, all night, pulling up at the traffic lights and then grinding away again. I nearly flipped. Honest I did. Didn't sleep for weeks – only in the mornings when I was too tired not to, or after half a bottle of spirits. And I had to be at school at eight o'clock in the morning two days a week. Eight o'clock! From November to March it was pitch dark.'

'You didn't try pills?'

I sensed the sidelong glance he threw me.

'No. I thought better not.'

This relieved me. When I first knew Maurice, he had been drugging quite a lot and I think I helped him break with it, or at least switch to alcohol.

'What happened then?'

'Well this girl at the Lycée, teacher of English, called Monique – Moni – realised I was going bonkers and ran a rescue operation. You'll like her if you get to meet her, though I doubt if you will now term's over. Her parents have this holiday flat in Biarritz and that's where I spent last night, and that's why I was able to meet you there. Anyway, she's awfully jolly and, you know, chummy, likes me gay, says she doesn't have to worry all the time if I am or am not going to get her knickers off, and found me this flat in the old part of town, in the centre. It's huge. Up four flights, no lift, did wonders for my figure. And after the *poids lourds* relatively quiet. Only two other inmates, both nice, Paul and Auguste.'

'I remember wondering why you had moved.' His only letter all year apart from two recent ones making and confirming arrangements for our summer trip, had been a note giving his new address. Just before Christmas.

'Well that's why. Because of the noise.'

As an account of what had gone wrong in his life in October and November this was skimped to say the least. It was three weeks before I heard a fuller version.

He went on: 'Paul is studying for his C.A.P.E.S. in English and is nice. Auguste is a *pétrolier* and absolutely bonkers.'

'*Pétrolier?*'

'He works on top of an oil derrick drilling for oil. There's an oil field near here, at Lacq. We'll pass it soon. He used to be a student but gave that up, then he was a burglar. Really. Lived off it for two years. Now he's a *derrickman*.' He gave the last word a comically French pronunciation. 'He works six weeks without a day off then two weeks holiday, and awful hours. Like from eight at night to four in the morning. He's two-handed, but has a skinny mad girlfriend at the moment, so I don't suppose he'll let you seduce him.'

I wanted to ask if this Auguste had taken him to bed, but couldn't bring myself to. Instead: 'So after a bad start all was well – lots of friends, lots of fun.'

'Yes. That's about it. More or less. There have been ups and downs of course,' and again something slightly shifty came into his tone and his expression too as far as I could see it. He was silent for a moment and then changed the subject, gave me an account of a film he had recently seen – *La Dernière Femme*, in which the hero ended it all by cutting off his whatsit with a Moulinex electric carver. 'Such a waste, he was really quite dishy, though with a tum almost as large as yours.'

Half an hour or so later we were in his shared flat: because no one was around Maurice showed me over it all, including the rooms of the other two occupants.

The kitchen was the largest room, and very large. In the corner furthest from the window a sink with a gas water heater, an old fashioned gas-fired hot water

26

radiator, a cooker, and an old and cheap sideboard, one of whose doors had been wittily painted round the holes that had been knocked in it. On the dirty walls behind, posters: an American eagle attacking a German vulture, recruiting World War I pilots; Chaplin; and an odd affair of large-booted, large-nosed characters tramping across a desert landscape with the legend 'Keep on Truckin!'.

There were tables, a stand-up clock case converted into a cupboard, and not only the walls were filthy. There was old food everywhere, mostly stale bread, but rotting vegetables, mildewed yoghourts as well.

'I'm surprised you don't have mice.'

'We do.' Maurice threw open the painted door of the sideboard and furry grey lightning scuttled away into a corner.

The other rooms weren't so bad. At the back under a sloping roof, was Auguste's. It had an oriental rug, a Napoleonic bed, a good desk, and was littered with fossils. A huge glass jar still held branches of japonica with a litter of very dead, two-month-dead flowers beneath. I sniffed. Maurice pouted.

'Yes, you're right. But he sticks with pot apart from the occasional pick-me-up. And I don't get invited often as he uses it mostly with his girl friend before beddy-byes.'

Paul's room was normal: just a bed, an armchair, no books.

'He's only here three nights a week; does all his serious work at St Jean de Luz where his girl friend has a pad.'

Maurice himself had two rooms, both small. The outer was littered with clothes, most of them dirty, all expensive. There was a spare couch. In the inner room his books, a large desk which also looked as if it might have been First Empire, and a large bed – double in fact.

'Er, I can sleep in the van,' I began, 'but if not I'll go and get . . .'

'Really Archie, don't be such a clammy knickers, of course you'll stay . . .'

And then the doorbell rang.

I waited in Maurice's outer room, heard voices, quick, in French, which I'm slow at, then steps down the corridor towards the kitchen. A moment later Maurice put his head round the door.

'You'd better come,' he said, suddenly pale again.

Puzzled I followed him.

In the kitchen a small wiry man with tightly curled short black hair stood up as we entered.

'Archie,' said Maurice, 'this is Paco Blas. He's a Spanish Basque and he wants us to smuggle him back over the border into Spain.'

CHAPTER 3

Two days later I was following this Paco at six thousand feet along a marked path on the side of a wide valley with the Lac de Gaube behind us and the massif of the Vignemale all of another four thousand feet and more above and ahead of us. Maurice trailed behind.

I was mildly surprised to find that I was enjoying myself quite considerably. I was not suffering, at least not yet, from altitude sickness, I was not finding it difficult to keep up with Paco though he must have been ten years younger, and of course the scenery was magnificent.

It was still only eleven o'clock in the morning – we had left Pau at eight – the sky was deep clear blue and the air crystal, almost luminous or luminiferous it seemed, so details stood out on mountains many miles away with the clarity one has experienced with certain hallucinogens. The only ominous sign, apart from this clarity, was what looked like the top of a huge pile of cloud peeping over the massif to the west, impossible to say how far away, or what height, or if it was likely to come our way – though probably it would: according to the Pau weather office the mountain weather had settled into a pattern of fine mornings and thunderous afternoons.

Meanwhile there was so much to enjoy. At Pont d'Espagne (twelve miles from the border in spite of the name) we had parked the van near a huge and exhilarating waterfall whose boom was indeed like the voice of doom. There followed a strenuous climb through pine forest up to the lake; now we were enjoying a relatively easy stroll first through more woods, then across meadows, and at last into a rockier landscape strewn with

29

boulders with patches of scree to cross where the valley narrowed. There were flowers everywhere, even in the tiniest rock crannies, and in the meadows unbelievably profuse and rich. I'm no expert on alpines but there were forget-me-nots, arctic rhododendron, elder-flowered orchid and marsh orchid, alpine squill, vetches, wild strawberry in fruit at the lower levels and in bloom higher up, bird's eye primrose, and – unbelievably since we were at the end of June – wild daffodil still in bloom right up near the foot of the Vignemale. And, above all (bother the pun), in the highest short-cropped grass, gentians – like fragments of lapis lazuli spilled on the ground by some passing Byzantine Emperor, too hard and pure in colour for any flower.

Maurice's sense of humour – rather contrived camp at the best of times – led him to invoke Julie Andrews and *The Sound of Music* in the lusher meadows, and this I found irritating: he sometimes teased me by professing to be turned on by hygienically jolly women. Still he did make me laugh when he thrust a handful of the appropriate herb beneath my nose and said with a conspiratorial leer: 'Hey Dad, what do you say to having a high old thyme with me, eh?'

It was good to find him cheerful again, for that first evening in the flat with Paco, and for much of the time since, he had been very and unaccountably miserable, although it seemed to me Paco had been at pains to reassure him.

'Maurice has got it wrong,' Paco had announced after shaking my hand – his palm dry, his grip unnaturally firm in the way of Americans who want to impress you. His English was American too and fluent, though he had a way of spacing out the words as if each one were carefully weighed and priced. 'Maurice expects that you shall stow me away in your motorised caravan, and take me over the border like hash or undeclared booze.'

'Well that is it, isn't it?' Maurice had said. 'I mean that is what you were asking me to lay on for you, isn't it?'

'Sure,' Paco had replied. 'Sure, that is what I asked. But I've been thinking it over since then, and well, I've been having second thoughts. Archie,' he went on, and took my elbow, looking up at me with dark brown eyes that remained hard in spite of the bonhomie, 'Archie will appreciate that.'

'I'm not sure I'm appreciating anything at the moment. Let me get this straight. You have already asked Maurice to ask me to get you into Spain in my van . . .'

'Correct.'

'And you are a Basque, a Spanish Basque, but *persona non grata* with the Spanish authorities.'

'*Persona non grata?* I like that. Yes I like that a lot. Archie, I am definitely not *persona grata* with the Franquista government over there; in fact if they caught me, identified me, they'd put me away for ten years. That's how far not *persona grata*.'

'A terrorist?'

Again the cold look, which I was beginning to think was meant to signal manly, serious frankness.

'No, Archie. Not a terrorist. That's a garrotting matter. Just a writer, editor, and publisher of a little clandestine literature here and there.'

Lid-er-a-chure, he said.

'Look, what he's done in Spain isn't the point,' Maurice had interrupted. 'Archie, I've got to say this, even though I've promised Paco that I'll try to persuade you to help him. We might get through. No doubt hundreds do. And English number plates and passports will help a lot. But if we're caught it could mean Spanish jail. At the best *we* could expect to be made *persona non grata* ourselves, and I'm meant to spend the summer in Spain . . .'

'Maurice . . .'

'Do you realise an innocent German tourist was shot dead last August, just because he failed to stop when a Civil Guard told him to? Do you realise . . . '

'Maurice. Let's get two things straight, shall we?' Paco's voice was firm and serious. 'Now I know you'll respect the promises you've made me, and I'll respect the promises I've made you . . . '

Of course I understood very little of all this at the time, but I could see that for a moment Maurice was frightened, frightened I now realise because he thought he had gone too far in persuading me to have nothing to do with Paco. But Paco went on, and a conciliatory tone crept into his voice.

' . . . and I've been trying to tell you that I don't want to go across in the van, or car, or whatever it is, at all. No, sir, not at all.'

There was silence for a moment, or did I fancy that I could hear the tiny scratching of a mouse behind the painted door?

'Well, that's a relief. That is a relief.'

'But that's not to say you can't help me still in a way that is much safer for all of us.'

And he had then gone on to explain what was apparently his revised plan, and it didn't seem so terrible.

First he cleared a large dirty bowl – the sort the French use for breakfast – off the table, wiped down the surface, then pulled from a pocket *Carte Numéro 2 du Parc National des Pyrénées* and a similar large scale map of the Spanish side.

'Big attraction for walkers – cross the border from a French refuge to a Spanish one, or vice versa. The fun of crossing borders with no customs post or police. This time of year, scores do it each day and with very little interference from the pigs – obviously if you've walked twenty, thirty kilometres you're not going to be carrying much contraband, and ninety-nine cases out of a hundred you'll be going straight back, same day or next day.

'Of course there are patrols, spot-checks – and that's why I'd like to have you along. You see, I've managed to get a passport, an Irish one, and it should do, it should do. But I'd feel happier if I had a coupla genuine Britishers along with me to chat up the Guards if they do pull us in – and that means you, fella,' he jabbed a friendly finger in Maurice's diaphragm. 'Since you speak Spanish so well, I shall be able to make out I'm just a dumb Mick who can scarcely manage his own language.'

And then he had gone on to show the route: up the Valley of the Gaube, over the Col des Oulettes which marked the border in the west of the Vignemale massif, down into the Valley of the Ara, and so to Torla where there were hotels, campsites, and hostels and where he expected to be able to mix in with the tourists, walkers, and climbers, and so disappear.

'The gr-r-reat thing is,' he had concluded, 'should it blow up on us, should some Guard question this passport or even recognise me, then you're still clear – at that point you can say I am a casual acquaintance, someone you've known only a day or two, and who asked if he could come along with you.'

'If it's going to be as easy as that for you, I don't see why you need us anyway,' Maurice had objected after a moment's thought.

'For protective colouring, and to speak Spanish. I thought I'd made that clear. Hell, why make such a deal of it? It'll be fun, an adventure for you, no harm. What do you say, Archie?'

I was ready to agree with him: he was a specious bastard, not without charm when he wanted. But what had not been made clear, what was still not clear now as we approached the Vignemale, was just why Maurice felt he had to help this Paco Blas. I had tried to get him to talk about it later that night after Paco had gone: he had not felt obliged out of political conviction, out of sympathy with the cause of Basque Separatism, I felt sure. Maurice is as apolitical as the Queen – whom I'm sure he admires almost as much as he does Julie Andrews. But he wouldn't say anything, brusquely snubbed me when I probed, and after nine months apart I had not wanted to provoke a squabble.

CHAPTER 4

Paco had called the next day, and surprised me, actually caused me some disquiet, by producing a wallet containing at least a thousand new francs with which he took us shopping. I know it held that much because that's what it cost to fit the two of us out with basic *randonnée* gear – fell boots, stockings, knickerbockers, anoraks, and rucksacks.

'Not only for your comfort,' Paco announced, 'but because we must be authentic if we are to outface the pigs.'

Now, as we struggled up the last and steepest slope to the Refuge des Oulettes I felt grateful – especially for the boots which were thick-soled with deep treads and heavy padding over and above the ankles; consequently my feet had suffered least. For, though in good condition – I hate to see a man of my age flabby and there is no excuse with the facilities that are available in the university – I was conscious of aching muscles in calves and thighs, and of the Col still far above us – a further twelve hundred feet.

The halt at the refuge was therefore welcome and not only because we needed the rest. The view was now quite magnificent: the Vignemale, the highest mountain in the French Pyrenees, stood across the valley floor in front of us, three huge pieces of rock – or perhaps one piece that had been split by aeons of frost – with a Y-shaped glacier separating the two smaller fragments from the larger; and then the sweep of the massif, a giant arc on either side of those giant peaks, like battlemented walls branching out from a keep or citadel. It was disconcerting to stare at such an immense object, and impossible to ignore it, even if one looked directly away, turned one's back on it;

disconcerting because the mind refused to accept its size and weight – it *had* to be two dimensional, a backdrop, an ephemeral projection merely on a screen of air or mist. To accept it as solid was to be forced to face up to volumes, surface areas, adamantine hardnesses and brittle cold, forced to accept sheer *weight* in thousands upon thousands of megatons, and then relate that weight to the whole globe it sat upon, smaller even than a blackhead on the back of Gargantua.

We sipped ice-cold beer from cans at fifty pesetas a throw, gazed at all this and now particularly at the col to the right, lower than the rest, and listened to the Refuge Keeper talk about the afternoon of storms ahead. Indeed, as we watched, the white cap of cloud I'd noticed earlier inched itself higher into the sky, began to show its grey and purple-black undersides suggestive of volumes of space even greater yet than the mountain it was drifting towards.

We were not alone. A group near us, two women with children, watched the rock faces a mile and a half away through binoculars, and muttered together monosyllabically. My eyes could not make out their men roped and nailed to vertical granite, but Maurice said he could see them. A little later, just before we left, another group of four men and two girls came across the valley floor towards us from the glacier's foot and flopped with a ringing rattle of pitons, crampons and picks at our feet. One of the women lowered her glasses and asked them how it was.

'Wet,' came the reply. 'Very wet. Slippery.' And the speaker returned to his boots which he unlaced with slow care, savouring the release as if it was a drink.

'Three Spaniards fell a month ago,' said Maurice in English, 'half way up the glacier. All killed.'

Paco up-ended his can and lobbed it into a bright blue plastic sack left out for rubbish.

'If we are to be in Torla by nightfall we must go,' he

said. 'Don't worry. This is not a climb we are going on, only a walk. There is no danger at all.'

As if to prove his point, two figures appeared silhouetted on the very col we were to make for, stood poised for a moment one foot in Spain and one in France, and then began the descent towards us. Paco was right – it looked steep, rocky, but walkable.

After twenty minutes Maurice complained. In that short time we had gone up perhaps five hundred feet and left the grass, indeed all living things except lichen, behind us. The path was no longer a path – simply a succession of widely spaced stones splashed with the red and white insignia of the *Parc* zig-zagging loosely up the steep slope of scree and rock above us. Looking back, the view down the valley had already opened up as if we were climbing in a helicopter, the folds and ridges flattened so that one was conscious now of space, the emptiness between us and the nearest similar height two miles or more away the other side of the refuge, and nothing, not even a bird, between.

'I don't like this,' said Maurice.

'It's tiring, no?' said Paco cheerfully. 'But in less than an hour we will be at the top, and then it is down hill all the way. A long way but down hill.'

He had not even looked round.

A little later the two we had seen on the col met and passed us; impassive and bearded with huge rucksacks, they tramped dourly by as if they carried the Tablets of the Law and were not yet too sure they would add to the sum of human happiness.

' *'Días,'* they muttered, and were gone.

I realised Maurice was lagging; for a moment or two the problem – whether to remain in contact with Paco or linger for Maurice – had an almost intellectual feel about it: one weighed up the alternatives as one weighs up some minutiae of literature, the possible meanings of a quibble in Donne, say, then Maurice's voice, more urgent now, brought the problem into sharper, more personal focus.

'Archie. Please stop.'

I turned and something near my heart melted. The poor boy was white, had gone forward on to his hands though from a purely physical point of view there was no need to at all, and was gripping the stones in front of him as though if he released them for a second he would go spinning out from the mountain-side like a space walker whose line is cut. I say "out" and not "down" for the gradient we were on was not as steep as a flight of stairs, and if he or any of us had taken even a nasty tumble a slither of more than ten feet was impossible. Enough to twist an ankle, take a nasty bruise or scrape, but no more. Yet the poor boy was obviously terrified out of his wits.

'I don't think I can go any further.'

'Paco? Paco!'

'Yes?'

'Something's wrong with Maurice.'

'Something's wrong? What's wrong?'

'I don't know.'

'Let's see what's wrong,' and the *soi-distant* Basque came clumping back down towards us dislodging a stone which, through an unlucky bounce or two, carried quite a long way before coming to rest. Maurice's eyes watched its course with widening horror.

'I'm frightened,' he moaned.

'But look, there is no danger. No danger at all. This is walking, not climbing. No ice; no snow even.'

'I'm sorry, but I'm frightened.'

'Why are you frightened? You are not sick are you?'

'If you mean do I feel as if I might heave up, the answer is yes. And dizzy too.'

'Perhaps he has vertigo,' I suggested.

'No, that is not possible. How can you have vertigo when there is no drop? Did he have breakfast?'

I thought back. Coffee with a lot of milk and sugar, hot bread with butter.

'Reasonable I should have thought.'

'Has he got a hangover? Did he drink much last night?'

Again I remembered. 'Yes,' I had to admit. 'We had half a bottle of *Izarra*.'

'*Joder,* that's it then. *Izarra* is strictly for the tourists. No Basque ever touches it. His stomach is upset a little, that is all. We shall have a rest, a little to eat, admire the view, and then we shall go on,' and he pulled bread and hard sausage from his rucksack and hacked out a rough sandwich with a clasp-knife.

With dreadful reluctance Maurice began to eat. I noticed that his eyes now never left the immediate fore-ground, our faces, his own hands; it seemed he would not even let them wander to his feet or the rock he was sitting on without their flinching away.

'Good. Now he feels better and we can go on.'

'Would you prefer it if you came between us?' I asked.

Dumbly he nodded.

As we continued to climb, I noticed that he was using his hands almost all the time and really it was almost never necessary. Also he dislodged a stone or two, one of which bumped against my shin.

'Watch it,' I called, and again he froze.

'Archie, I really don't think I can take any more of this.'

Again Paco galumphed back to us.

'Maurice, you must tell me what is the matter.'

'I'm bloody scared, I'm scared out of my mind, I think I'm going to slip.'

'You will not slip. You cannot slip. But you are far more likely to slip if you lean forward into the slope, and that is why you keep dislodging stones. Look. It's a simple matter of gravity.' He demonstrated. 'If you are upright, your weight pushes the stones down to the centre of the earth, not to the valley floor. But if you lean, the line of force is parallel to the slope and so of course you slip and make the scree move too. Now take my hand and stand upright.'

39

'Sod your lines of force. Leave go. For Christ's sake, leave me alone.'

There was a moment's silence. Dimly I was aware of more passion beating around me than I understood.

Then there was a new noise, a sudden splatter of heavy rain drops and a gust of wind. Distantly thunder rumbled. I looked up. The sky immediately above was black, though there was still plenty of blue elsewhere, even behind the peaks of the Vignemale itself.

'Come,' said Paco. 'We shall get a soaking else.'

'Archie, I don't have to, do I?' The plea was agonising, though incomprehensible.

'No, of course you don't if you don't want to,' I replied.

'But I think he does,' Paco's face was more blank, the eyes harder than I had seen before.

'Why?'

The argument had shifted: it was between the Basque and me now, with Maurice watching helplessly. The rain began to fall steadily – cold, on a wind, and thunder barged about the peaks behind us, already closer.

'Why? Because I need someone who will speak Spanish if I am stopped; so I can maintain the pretence that I am Irish. I explained all this.'

'But it doesn't have to be Maurice.'

'Doesn't it? I think so. Maurice knows why.'

We turned back to him. Rain was streaming down his ashen face mixed, I suspected, with tears. He had begun to shiver.

'I can't, Paco. I can't go on.' He was shaking his head with an emphasis one could not possibly ignore. 'You just don't know how frightened I am. I don't think I can get down, let alone go on. Do what you like, I can't go on.'

Again the rain and the thunder. What did he mean by 'Do what you like'?

Paco resolved it at last. 'All right. All right, I shall

40

chance it on my own. You shall have to get down as best you can, but I am going on.'

He gave his rucksack a hitch, thrust his hands into his pockets, and stumped off up over the rocks and scree. In a moment or two he was out of sight and the thunder crashed suddenly right overhead. The rain became a torrent, the upper slopes of the Vignemale to our right disappeared behind cloud, though the glacier still gleamed whitely through.

Going down was a desperate business. For most of the time Maurice insisted on clutching my arm or shoulder which made balance difficult on the now wet stones; hysteria is catching – I began to share his sense of the emptiness in front of us, the horror of the chasm of air and rain between us and the mountain opposite. At least I now had an inkling of the state he had got himself into – an inkling too, of what you must have suffered here in Santiago, dear Maurice, on the roof of the Cathedral.

CHAPTER 5

I had him back to the flat in Pau by about half-past six; made him take a bath (in the large sit-down affair – hip-bath? – which I had to clean out first, it was filthy) and then we went out for a steak in the restaurant round the corner. Nothing special, though the local soup, *garbure*, was more pleasant than its name suggests. The poor lad nearly fell asleep over his Grand Marnier. As I put him to bed I could hear voices from the kitchen and since it seemed he had gone straight to sleep, and I still felt wakeful, I decided to go along and introduce myself.

Actually, we had got a bit on edge with each other during the bath, and the flavour of the tiff still lingered. It had been my fault: soaping him I had been carried away somewhat – his skin is like . . . well, all the obvious things smooth white skin is like – and one thing led to another, and he just wasn't in the mood. Silly of me to expect him to be, after what he had been through.

The awful kitchen was dense with acrid tobacco smoke. Three girls were ranged along the bench behind the table, a young man in spectacles and a white bathrobe sat at the end. The geyser was roaring and the bath next door was refilling. The youth was just finishing a large helping of raw, untreated, ground steak; he pushed the plate away and pulled in a bowl filled with a brown-grey mush I later guessed to be banana, honey and yoghourt, and this too he shovelled in with marvellous voracity. All three girls were talking and smoking and for a moment none of them registered my presence. Since they were speaking quickly and in student argot I had no idea what they were talking about; I had time to take them in.

At the end of the row was Monique (later I sorted out their names) – large eyes, bumpy nose, shortish curly fair hair. She was wearing a lot of makeup round her eyes and rouge on her cheeks, an embroidered cheesecloth top which left a rather skinny breastbone exposed, six long necklaces, eight rings, a three-quarter skirt, and boots. Then Lili – very short, pert face, older than the others, very large sweater with a huge halter neck – much too big for her. Finally Jeanne-Marie – of skeletal thinness, gaunt, staring eyes whose frequent smile was always belied by the downward droop of her mouth. She was wearing a bottle-green cord suit, more jewellery than an English girl would ever wear but less than Monique, brown boots.

Auguste, for the man was he – the ex-burglar der-rickman – now stood up, belched loudly and lengthily, and said: 'You are Eeenglish, no? I go to take a bath,' and he went.

Monique turned to take me in, as if she had only then become aware of my presence. She was smoking through a holder and I should have thought her affected if I had not been immediately impressed by the extraord-inary openness of her expression, of her eyes especially. I think she was incapable of real affectation – anything that looked like it must be a put-on, a game, in this case 'dressing-up'.

'You must be Maurice's friend. He told us that he was expecting you.'

Her English was good; slightly nasal and careful perhaps.

'Yes. My name is Archie. Archie Connaught.'

And we all shook hands: Monique with her wide look of utter frankness, Lili with a chirpy grin that held a lot of flirtation, Jeanne-Marie with disdain, or at any rate with-out any show of interest.

'Won't you have a coffee? Where is Maurice?'

'Thank you. He's in bed and asleep I think; he has had a trying day.'

43

'Tiring or trying?'

I found myself explaining the difference, and then most of the circumstances that led up to Maurice's mild collapse.

Monique made two significant comments. The other two had little English: Lili occasionally murmured a question to Monique; Jeanne-Marie ignored us, staring into space and smoking with intensity. The heavy charm bracelet on her wrist occasionally chimed with impatience.

'It is very strange,' Monique said, 'that Maurice should go for a walk in the mountains, a walk of that sort up the side of a mountain. He came with us in October and was very frightened then too, and it is strange he should go again.'

'Perhaps he had not realised we would go so high above the valley on such a steep slope,' I suggested.

'Maybe,' but she continued to shake her head and purse her lips.

Her other comment was more emphatic. 'I do–an't like Paco Blas. No, I'm sorry but I don't like him. Why? I don't know. There is something. I just don't like him.'

A little later Auguste came bouncing back among us. He was dressed now in a dark shirt, a floppy sweater, tight jeans. His hair was wet, he looked clean, lively, full of energy, rather attractive in a butch sort of way. I guessed the bath would be filthy again.

'Now,' he announced, after a false start in argot: he switched to his execrable English at a word from Monique, 'now we shall go drinking. Today I was on the top of, how you say, rig? Oil-rig. Derrick. The lightning it came, the thunder. The rain. It is thirty metres. Thirty metres up, you know? I think I am very lucky man to be alive, very lucky. Because I am lucky I want to play. At the casino. But Jeanne-Marie, she say no. So tonight we drink, and no play . . .'

Feeling warmed by their company and cheerfulness I

went back down the passage to see if Maurice was awake. He was, but only just. His speech, coming out of the darkness of his bed, was slurred. I suspected that he had taken something.

'No. No. I won't come. But you go if you want. You go. But don't come back pissed. Or anyway, don't wake me up if you do.'

The five of us squeezed into Lili's Mini and drove down to El Bolero, an imitation Spanish restaurant in the Hédas, the ravine that bisects Pau; it used to be an open sewer and is even now a rather seedy area spanned by bridges which keep the smarter part of the town clear of it. But El Bolero was all right, quite fun really – candle-lit, small, bull-fight posters – there must be hundreds of thousands of places like it, in Spain as well as everywhere else. The three girls shared a huge bowl piled with rice and shellfish – langoustine, mussels, clams and giant prawns – which Auguste and I, having eaten already, picked at whenever they let us. We all drank a great deal of red Spanish wine.

Two episodes in the conversation turned out to have some importance. During the discussion of what was to be done with *Les Vacances*, Monique said that she and Lili were planning to 'make autostop' to Lisbon: both shared romantic ideas about the revolution there. First they were taking in Pamplona for San Fermín.

'But why not go in Lili's car?' I asked.

'Oh, I have much fear to conduct in Spain,' said Lili with wide eyes and shaking head.

Jeane-Marie said something with her mouth full: it seemed that she thought that the real reason was that they would find it easier to find the right sort of holiday boyfriends if they were hitchhiking, than if they themselves were giving the lifts. About the holidays she and Auguste had not decided – Auguste would have only his fortnight and that was not due for another three weeks.

45

Then Monique told Auguste about our misadventure in the mountains with Paco Blas.

'*Merde!*' he cried. 'That Paco Blas is a, how you say, Moni, *comment on dit "un con"?*'

She told him.

'Also,' he went on, 'he is not a Basque. That I know.' He tapped the side of his nose. 'And he has some very nasty friends. I know also the reason for why Maurice does all these things for Paco. But I no tell you. I no tell you.'

Which was a pity since it was a question I wanted to know the answer to.

There was another question which did not occur to me, though I find it incredible now that it did not. And that is – just what was Paco Blas up to? It had seemed a desperately important matter for him to get into Spain in an unofficial way. To do this he had procured an Irish passport, and had in some way or other coerced Maurice's co-operation. Yet when Maurice baulked on the mountain face and Paco was left to walk into Spain alone and more or less openly, he had simply gone on, as if there was no problem at all. Why? Why not turn back with us and concoct another way of doing it? After all it would surely have been easy enough to drive east or west and find a crossing with less vertiginous slopes.

I should have considered these questions. The answer was simple enough: it was not the actual crossing that was important to Paco but that we should know that he had made it. If I had worked that out, then Maurice might not now be strapped up with tubes up his nose and in his arm, and his heart and breathing wired into a thing like a television monitor. I left him half an hour ago: there has been little or no improvement in his condition.

PART TWO

Pamplona

CHAPTER 6

'Thank God for that,' said Maurice, as we drove down the steep hill from the Col du Somport, from the customs post and into Spain.

'Why? Because we're through all right?' I always feel nervous at customs, even when I have nothing to fear at all.

'Oh no. Because we are out of bloody France and into Spain. I can breathe here.'

'Was it so rough in Pau?'

'Oh, most of the time it was great. But there were problems. Quite bad ones, and now they're over and done. It's gone. All left behind. Thank God.'

'To do with Paco Blas?'

'To do with who the hell cares what. It's over. So there's no need to pump me about it. But I could cheer because we'll never see that bastard again. Hey, look at that. Isn't that marvellous?'

I thought he was talking about the view. We had just negotiated a steep bend in the middle of what looked to be a rather smart ski resort, and a mountain panorama, more bare of trees, less claustrophobic than on the French side, had opened out in front of us. But it was the road sign he was looking at.

It said *Camino de Santiago. Jaca 28. SANTIAGO 736* and it was decorated with a scallop shell emblem.

'Yes, of course. The Pilgrims' Way.'

'You know about it?'

'Naturally: "At Rome she hadde been, and at Boloigne, In Galice at Seint Jame, and at Coloigne." '

'Who?'

'The Wife of Bath.'

'Do you know the whole of the *Prologue* to *The Canterbury Tales* by heart?'

'Yes.'

'Christ!'

I drove on feeling slightly smug – it may not be an important achievement and I don't actually learn verse that easily, but it's something I feel one ought to do.

'Archie, have you got a calendar?'

'There's one, a plastic card, in the document box.'

When travelling in my van I keep all the papers, passports, green card and so on in an old cash box.

'Yes. I thought so, and this is rather great.'

'What?'

'This year the twenty-fifth of July falls on a Sunday, and when that happens it's a Holy Year at Santiago.'

'So?'

'Well it's the National Day anyway you know – Saint James being Patron of Spain and all that. But when it comes on a Sunday it's a big deal. Hey, I bet the King'll turn up.'

'The King?'

'Juan Carlos, stupid. It'll be a ball. Hey, Archie, we can go, can't we?'

'What, after Pamplona? I don't see why not. You know it's coming back to me now. The B.B.C. had a good documentary on it three, four years ago. The Ministry of Tourism has opened up the old route and sign-posted it the whole way so if you follow it you go past all those rather good Romanesque churches. That sign back there must have been the first of them. Yes. Let's do that. Pilgrims on the jolly old Camino.'

'We'll have to have floppy hats, scallop shells, staffs, and gourds, what fun!'

 ' "Give me my scallop shell of quiet,
  My staff of Faith to walk upon,
  My scrip of joy, immortal diet,
  My bottle of Salvation . . ." '

'Archie?'

'Yes?'

'I hope you're not going to spout verse at every opportunity. Curb the habit occasionally, eh?'

And so we drove on down into Jaca, in a rather jolly mood. I must say I liked the thought that that terrible old butch bag, the Wife, had wandered 'by the weye' down this very road, on her 'amblere', in her red stockings and hat as broad as a shield. 'Gat-toothed was she' – sign of lechery, and good luck to her, fancying the legs of her husband's apprentice even while the lad was carrying her husband's coffin.

I have nothing to say to those who object that the Wife of Bath is a fictional character.

In Jaca we went to the tourist office and picked up some pamphlets about the Holy Year and the Camino de Santiago and read them in a nice pub where they grilled lamb chops over an open fire for us.

'I love Jaca,' said Maurice. 'I came over whenever I could, but could only manage it three times. Don't you think it's peaceful, normal, *civilised*, after all the rush and bother in France?'

And the booze is a lot cheaper, I thought, as he sloshed himself another glass of the really very pleasant wine out of the jug in front of us. He had two *coñacs* with his coffee and slept most of the way to Pamplona, but not before he'd gone into ecstasies over the new twenty-five peseta piece that came with the change.

'It's the first I've seen,' he crowed. 'Oh, can I have it, Archie? Let me keep it.'

Of course I passed it across.

'Look at him. Juan Carlos Primero, Rey de España,' he read. 'That's all. And on the other side, let's see. Just a crown and veinticinco pesetas. Isn't that marvellous? After forty years under that filthy murderer, with his evil face on every coin and stamp, and his fascist insignia

51

everywhere, isn't that marvellous?'

'I thought most Spaniards reckon he's just the same old thing again. The King, I mean.'

'Oh the Lefties do, and the Basques, I daresay. But the Right is a lot more worried about him than the Left. He's a good bloke, I think. I really do. And it'll be jolly nice if he does go to Galicia for Saint James's Day, and I bet he will.'

Another thunderstorm (and by no means the last of that first fortnight in July) impressively heralded our arrival at Pamplona, and indeed woke Maurice up. I could see the clouds huge, dense, and purple from up to thirty miles east of the town when we were still crossing the wide open plain of the Aragón (we had passed its source close to that Camino de Santiago sign in the high Pyrenees) and when at last the town itself came clearly into view the storm broke with shattering claps of thunder, forked lightning all over the place, and a cloudburst. Although I did not know it at the time, the drought remained unbroken in England.

'Christ, what's that?' said Maurice coming to with a start.

'The beginning of San Fermín by the look of it.'

'It's rather grand, isn't it?'

'Lucky we can sleep in the van. I wouldn't fancy putting up a tent in this lot.'

'No indeed.'

What we did have to do was buy tickets for the bullfights. A pamphlet we had picked up at Jaca said that that evening, the fifth of July, was the last occasion one could book in advance – thereafter only a few places kept back were sold on the night preceding each fight. Thus, by arriving on the fifth we hoped to buy tickets for the four out of the total of nine fights that Maurice, who was something of an *aficionado*, wanted to see.

But it didn't work out like that. I managed to park the

van outside the bullring all right, and we were in the very long queue by half-past four – more or less sheltered by the large plane trees outside the Plaza de Toros; all seemed to be going well. But as we inched forward a notice over the ticket booths announced by stages that each day was sold out: *No hay billetes para días 14, 11, 13.* Then a little later the figures *10, 12, 8* were added and so on until by the time our turn had arrived the only tickets left were for the *novillada*, apprentice bullfight, on the sixth. We bought seats for that and went back to the van. It was still raining.

'What now?' asked Maurice.

'Find somewhere out in the country where we can park off the road, have something to eat, read a book, go to bed.'

'Great. It's not like that in Hemingway.'

'No. Look, shall we make a bargain about Hemingway?'

'Not to mention him again? Fine. He's not really much good, is he?'

'He's a very good writer who was not at his best on bull-fighting or old men in small boats.'

'If the subject is to be taboo, we'll do without your lecture notes.'

We parked in a field about five miles out, ate out of tins, and drank too much. We soon got rather bad-tempered with each other. It continued to rain.

53

CHAPTER 7

The next day was awful.

It was still raining at dawn and went on raining until three o'clock and so we missed the rocket. ('The only explosion in that greatest of all war novels is the rocket that signals the opening of the fiesta — ' see almost any crit of the between wars American novel, ref. Hemingway, op. cit., passim, et seq., etc.) We missed it because it was the sixth of July and everyone knows that San Fermín is the seventh – but Maurice had forgotten that Spanish fiestas always begin on the Eve. That, at any rate, was the only way I could shift the blame back on to him.

'After all, you're meant to be the Spanish expert.'

'Yes, but it's you who reads the guide books and arranges everything.'

It was one o'clock then and I had just found in the official programme that the rocket had gone up at twelve. It wasn't the best year to see it anyway – the first rocket in rain for forty years. Which meant that the last in rain had been eleven days before Franco rebelled, and this was the first after Franco's death.

At three the sky began to brighten and it looked as if there would be a *novillada* after all. It wasn't due to start until a quarter to eight but by now we were tired of nothing but each other's company and so we decided to return to the town. Of course, the van stuck. I had parked in a meadow (refreshingly green after the outfield at Lord's) and at the foot of a short slope nicely screened from the road by trees; the soil was soft, the thick grass slippery. It took us about twenty minutes to get out though no harm was done except to our trousers and our tempers.

The town was bleak: the streets and buildings looked grey, black and wet; the crowds were beginning to gather after the siesta, beginning to drink, beginning to bang drums and blow bugles, but all with a slightly desperate determination. Now and again the rain returned, but only as a drizzle. The seedy atmosphere was exacerbated by a rash of black and red slogans sprayed on to most walls – they called for a popular assembly for Navarra, for amnesty, and many were in Basque, all 'x's, 'gu's, 'tl's, and double 'r's.

Maurice got excited about these: they were a symptom of the thaw after Franco, he said. No doubt anyone caught at it would be shot on sight by a Guardia (a youth was shot dead in Alicante for just this at the end of the month) but they showed that people thought that it was worth sloganising, that something might come of it: unthinkable eight months ago.

He picked up a handout or rather throwaway – later we saw people 'distributing' these leaflets: the method was to drop a handful and walk briskly away. This one was in Basque and Spanish; declared itself for amnesty, liberty, 'popular' fiestas, and Basque independence; it condemned the crimes of Montejurra and ended with 'Down with the Dictatorship'. It had been printed by a group called the LCR-ETA VI which appeared from its insignia to be an extreme left-wing organisation.

Maurice said he would make a collection of such things (he called them *realia*) for his language work next term, and suggested that I could take photographs of the slogans.

'Should please Stukely and the rest of them,' he added. 'They're all raving commies.'

'What are the crimes of Montejurra?' I asked.

'I don't know. We must try to find out.'

Without particularly intending to, we found ourselves outside the town hall. A noisy crowd had gathered in the small square which, with its façades ornamented in the

Spanish sixteenth-century style known as plateresque, has more grace about it than most of Pamplona. We stopped to see what was going on. The crowd became thicker and a sort of flow became noticeable; what was happening was that large groups of youths were passing through about a hundred at a time, all dressed alike in white shirts, white trousers, espadrilles with red laces, and red three-cornered scarves round their necks. Each group had a large banner painted with cartoon figures and a band of drums and bugles. They halted in front of the Town Hall and made a huge noise which always culminated with the shouted syllables *riau*, *riau*, *riau*, with both arms raised and the hands twisted on each *riau*. I felt a touch of fiesta spirit with these *riaus*, though my feet were still cold.

'Who are all these chaps in white?' I asked.

'The *peñas*, clubs of bullfight supporters. Mostly working-class, and they do charity work as well.'

A proper band now appeared, and we heard for the first time the song that was to haunt us throughout the month – 'Ramona'. A verse about how this good-time girl came to Pamplo-o-o-na was repeated again and again with absurd enthusiasm by the crowd.

Finally the Mayor and Corporation appeared in top hats and frock coats, with the Guardia Civil carrying machine guns in attendance. We consulted the programme.

'It's a procession up to the Cathedral for the sung vespers of San Fermín,' said Maurice.

'Really? I'm cold and could do with a drink.'

We were but two of thirty thousand or so with the same idea. We tried three bars up the Estafeta, the narrow mediaeval street where most of the more picturesque bars are, but the struggle to get through the noisy, pushy mob in front of each counter, the difficulty in persuading the barmen to charge us fairly for two red wines, were all too much for me and I suggested we go back to the van, and have a sandwich and a beer while we waited for the bullfight.

'The trouble is you're not in festival mood,' Maurice commented, rather sulkily. 'I have known times when you'd go out of your way to be jostled by burly Spanish peasants.'

'It needs sun,' I replied shortly.

Sandwiches were off: no bread, and as of the sixth of July and for the next eight days shops would open in the mornings only.

I think it was while we were trying to find an open *panadería* that I first became conscious of the Anglo-Saxon element in the crowd – mostly American and Australian it seemed, some Scandinavians, very few British.

The men tended to be huge in comparison with the Spaniards – fair, fat, moustached. They carried gin bottles in their hip pockets and swigged from them at five-minute intervals. The girls wore long dresses, beads, had long hair, and seemed sluttish. Both sexes affected bare feet in flip-flops which looked wretched in the soggy garbage that the rain had collected in the gutters. All were wet and drunk, most of them sourly, aggressively drunk. One overheard occasional snatches of · conversation: 'This is the greatest since Rio', 'Did you get your places for the corr-eee-da? You did? That's fine', 'Ginny here has already vomited three times, but she doesn't mean to give up, do you Ginny? Not give up, just throw up; hey, did you hear that? I just made a funny – Ginny never gives up, just throws up; hey, Bill did you hear the funny I just made . . . ', and so on.

Maurice was right: I was not in fiesta mood.

A group of these Anglo-Saxons sat in front of us at the bullfight. They were: an American couple with a small girl aged five, and two Norwegian youths about Maurice's age. They talked in English. The little girl kept up a barrage of inane questioning throughout the first two bulls, to which she got equally inane and hopelessly inaccurate answers. When the third bull came in, her father (now I think of it I've no evidence for saying he was her father and judging from their apparent lifestyle I shouldn't think he had either), her putative father said: 'The last two didn't stand much of a chance, did they? But this one looks stronger – perhaps we'll see the bull win this time.'

This was too much for me in the black mood I was in.

'For Christ's sake,' I said, 'a bullfight is not a competition to see who wins. It's not even a fight. A matador who gets hurt is a bad matador, at least at that particular moment.'

I said this as rudely as I could, hoping to shut them up.

'Say, is that so? Now that is a truly interesting angle on the whole business. We don't know a whole lot about it and we sure would be grateful if you'd talk us through this one, wouldn't we, honey?'

Maurice butted in before a properly offensive reply had formed itself in my mind.

'Pay no attention to him,' he said, 'he's in a grumpy mood, and anyway understands very little more of what's going on down there than you do,' and he proceeded to give the commentary they had asked for. I must admit he did it rather well.

When it was all over – it was a pretty poor affair with weak bulls and young matadors not fully established, who were full of crowd catching tricks and false bravado – it was naturally suggested that we should have a drink together.

'We know a great little bar on the city walls, near the cathedral; we sure would like you to come along there with us,' the girl said. She was a mousy thing, in regulation mud-spattered long skirt and beads. Her child was dressed almost identically, and both had dirty faces.

Along the battlements, things were so contrived that I

58

walked with the Americans while Maurice and the Norwegians came behind; they were blond, tall, wore shorts – which is practically an obscenity in Spain off a beach – and were undeniably pretty. One of them particularly so with pale yellow down on his thighs and a soft downy moustache to match.

The American kid began to holler. 'Look Momma, look Momma, you c'n see down, down, down to our tent. You can, Mom, come'n see,' so we all joined her on the wall and looked down into the park below, Maurice giving notice of his vertigo with a shudder. The place was filled with caravans, tents, vans – an unnofficial though tolerated camp-site.

'It's a bit rough,' the American admitted. 'You know, everyone craps where they want to so you have to watch where you put your feet, but, hell, you expect to rough it in Spain.'

No Spaniard would ever live thus – as a nation they are as fastidious as cats.

The bar they took us to was an attractive place with low vaulted ceilings and a pleasant window with coloured glass overlooking a patio garden lit with fairy lights. It was not unbearably crowded and the *tapas*, bar snacks, looked appetising. We were hungry and broke the Spanish custom of the *chateo* or pub-crawl by staying for more than one round.

After I'd brought over the third lot from the bar – three wines for me and the Americans, one Coca-Cola for the little girl, and three *cuba libres* for the boys – I went to the lav. When I came back there were two Americans, one small girl, and three empty glasses.

'They just went,' said the American.

'They just smiled, told us good night, and blew,' said his wife. If she was his wife.

'Do you know them? The Norwegians, I mean.'

'Never saw them before this evening.'

'I mean are they camping down near you?'

'We haven't seen them down there, have we, honey? But there's lots of folks down there and maybe that's where they're at.'

'If you see them again, Maurice that is, tell him I've gone back to our van. He knows where it is. By the bullring.'

'Sure. Will do. I get it – Maurice is *your* friend. OK, we'll pass on the message if we see them.'

I made my way back to the bullring through streets that were beginning to take on a nightmarish aspect. Gangs of white clad youths from the *peñas* bombed up and down, arm in arm, blowing those things that uncurl and make a raspberry noise. Large men with large hands and large stomachs dragged their families behind them from bar to bar with mothers equally large and fat in black, with five or six children all immaculately groomed but a little pale, a little wondering; the restaurants were filling up for the late Spanish supper – waiters pushing between crowded tables carried platters of fried chicken and jugs of wine. The only scruffs were the gypsies – hanging on your sleeve, pointing plaintively at the wizened babies in their arms; and the foreigners who here and there had succumbed in a doorway or on a bench. Bottles rattled and broke in the gutters.

Near the bullring cheers and shouts, screams of delighted fear and a quick succession of reverberating explosions: above the heads of the crowd the black silhouette of a bull bobbing and swaying while crackers, Roman candles, small rockets, whizz-bangs exploded from its sides and from between its horns, showering the children around with sparks so the air smelled of singed hair and the ears were lacerated with percussions. For one awful moment in the swinging mixture of intense dark and sudden light the bull seemed real, alive, but near to was seen to be an object not unlike a gymnastic horse carried by a running man hidden beneath it, and festooned with fireworks.

60

The van was parked right against the bullring. A man was urinating against the wall with his backside resting on the bonnet. He heard me unlock the door, turned and said something cheerily at me as he buttoned up, and then, when I didn't answer, leant nearer – his teeth were bad and his eyes bleary – 'Americano?' he suggested, 'Alemán? Francés?'

'Inglés.'

'Inglés? Ay haf go in Sowd-am-don,' he took my shoulder and I felt his weight as his knees sank. 'Ay haf go in Sow-dam-don.'

I managed to shrug him off, get in, and shut the door. He shouted, banged on the side of the van, and staggered off singing something that might have been *ee-i-addio we won the Cup,* but I don't suppose it was.

I opened a tin of soup but it wasn't much fun without bread. I didn't want any more to drink; sleep was out of the question: the noise showed no sign of abating; the *chateo* or *paseo* looked like going on till dawn, a *peña* band went by and some Australians singing 'Waltzing Matilda'. I tried to read, but that meant leaving the light burning: drunks loomed up, peered in, faces distorted by booze and shadows; I felt like Cousteau in a diving bell.

With the lamp off, fantasies flooded in out of the darkness. Where was Maurice? What was happening to him? What were they *doing* to him? (A touch of the green-eyed monster in this one.) But mainly, genuinely, was he all right? The conviction grew – no, he was not, not all right; not with his inclinations, his weaknesses, not loose in Pamplona on the Eve of San Fermín.

I scrawled a note: *Maurice, it is eleven o'clock. I will be back here at half past twelve. WAIT HERE. Love Archie* and left it under the windscreen wiper.

Where to start? I thought for a moment and then headed for the unofficial camp-site outside the walls: at least the Americans might be back now, they would be able to tell me is they had come across him. It wasn't difficult to find. Some wag had used a spray can on the road signs and written in English: ORGY THIS WAY, with arrows. The park itself was dark apart from a tented bar where ten Australians were drinking beer – a lot of beer, there must have been a hundred bottles lined up on the counter in front of them. Around in the shadows, tents, guy ropes to trip on, one or two caravans and cars, a lot of converted commercial vans like mine, but older and in worse condition. An overpowering smell of stale drink, urine, with here and there the sharpness of vomit. A child was crying, bodies heaved, humped, and moaned beneath canvas, behind thin steel walls. Odd phrases floated out of the darkness: 'You filthy bitch', and a spluttered giggle; 'No honestly I've nothing against blacks, it's just that I never yet have had one', 'I don't know why the bastard hit me.' There was no sign of Maurice, Norwegians, or the American trio.

Back in the town I passed the *verbena* in the Taconera Gardens: dancing, open-air bars, paper lanterns that had somehow survived the rain. It looked jolly, but definitely a night out for the family, not Maurice's scene. Nor was the *baile popular* in the main square where five thousand people bounced up and down in what passes for dancing on such occasions, to the music of two competing trumpeters with electronic backing. It sounded like Sousa in Latin-American rhythm.

There remained the Estafeta and the warren of similar streets with countless bars between the Plaza and the Cathedral. With growing despair and disgust I made my way into the area, admitting what I had known all along, that this is where they would be.

The alleyways were now a litter of refuse – half-eaten sandwiches, chicken bones, smashed melons, soggy loaves, and bottles of every shape and size. There were drunks everywhere, and in every stage of intoxication from the more or less upright and bellicose, through the weavers and totterers, to the actually fallen. This last group subdivided into those who could still sit and drink, and those who were flat out on their backs or, as often as not, their fronts.

The bars were emptier now, the clientele almost entirely foreign. I had two false alarms: I followed one trio of youths down into a basement toilet before satisfying myself that Maurice was not one of them; I disturbed a couple fondling in a doorway – the dark haired half turned out to be a girl in jeans.

At last I reached a small square near the Cathedral. There was a small fountain, not playing, in the middle and rather more street lighting than there had been. It was filled with foreigners, nearly all sitting and mostly staring ahead out of glazed eyes from faces waxy and pale. Near the fountain two bearded characters in leather cowboy hats strummed guitars. They had neither technique nor inspiration. The tune they were attempting was 'Blowing in the Wind'. Near to them I found Maurice and one of the Norwegians, the one with the downy moustache.

Maurice was a mess. Sitting with his back against the fountain his hair, which he was normally proud of, was filthy, and his soft leather jacket was torn – or at least one sleeve was coming away from the shoulder. His eyes were open but did not seem to see much, his skin was clammy to touch. Between his knees was a litre spirit bottle, three quarters empty, the liquor was cherry-red.

The Norwegian was not so far gone. He blinked at me, focused, and then nodded – more to himself than to me.

'Your friend,' he said. 'Good. He cannot walk, I am thinking.'

'No? Perhaps you can help me.'

'No. Also I am not walking.'

'Well, I think we should try.'

'Oh yes. Everyone shall . . . is . . . may try.'

He pulled himself up an inch or two and then slipped back.

63

'It is not so easy,' he said.

'Look. I'll try and find some coffee.'

Gently I pulled the bottle away from between Maurice's thighs – for a second his fingers tightened on it, then relaxed. *Pacharán*, the label said. It smelled of anis. As I straightened, one of the leather-hatted guitarists reached out a hand and took it from me. He swigged, gagged, dropped it. It smashed in the gutter.

'Thanks, Dad,' he said.

My Spanish was just about up to persuading a waiter from a nearby café to bring out two large black coffees. He stood and watched, immaculate in black trousers and white jacket with a slight frown of disapproval between his brows, while I coaxed the pair of them to drink up.

'*Ciento cincuenta,*' he murmured as I returned the cups to his zinc tray.

I gave him two hundreds. Pedantically he fiddled out a fifty-peseta piece from the waistcoat beneath his jacket. I took it: one doesn't tip in Spain, and, with a falling pound, he had already charged me sixty pence a cup.

I managed to get them on their feet. The Norwegian could just about walk, Maurice not at all, not on his own. With him in the middle the three of us began to weave our way back to the bullring.

Ramo-o-ona . . . ya-ta-ta-ta, ya-ta-ta Pamplo-o-ona, went the crowd and the band in the Plaza.

'Where's your friend?' I asked the Norwegian.

'My friend? Ah. Henrik. He became angry and went . . . not home. How shall I say? Back to where we stay.'

'Why was he angry?'

'Because Maurice tried to kiss him. We are not . . . like that. Maurice thought so. My friend became angry and went away.'

'Why did you stay?'

'Because I am thinking Maurice should not be being alone.'

64

'Thank you. That was kind.'

A little later, quite near the van, just by the bullring, we paused for a moment in front of a bronze bust set on a square granite plinth. The head was round, the metal beard neat and trimmed.

'After all,' said my Norwegian, 'if it was not for him, perhaps we would not be here. It is his fault.'

Because of the play of shadows from the plane trees I could not read the inscription. I did not need to. I had already noted that we were at the end of the *Paseo de Hemingway*.

CHAPTER 8

'Where are we going?' The voice was weak but petulant; it came from the bunk behind the driver's seat.

'The coast,' I replied. The traffic was heavy, I was trying to spot a turning to the left that would cut out the bottle-neck at Tolosa.

'But what about Pamplona? San Fermín?'

'I think we've had enough of San Fermín for a bit.'

'But it's only just started.'

'If you're good, and promise to stay good, we'll go back for the last day or two.'

There followed a longish patch of silence, perhaps five minutes.

Then: 'Was I very naughty?'

'Yes.'

Another pause.

'You'll have to tell me. Tell me how naughty.'

'I don't think I'm exaggerating to say that you are lucky to be alive. And certainly lucky not to be in prison.' With a punch on the horn I swung out, overtook a cattle-truck and a Coca-Cola van.

'I must say I feel rotten now. But lucky to be alive?'

'Look. I found you out of doors, scantily clad, it was a damp and chilly night. Because of this, but more because of the amount of alcohol you had consumed, you were suffering from the early stages of hyperaesthesia: I think that's the right term.'

'Hyperthermia.'

'At all events you were very cold, and once you were back here continued to complain of the cold. You actually said, two or three times, that you thought you were dying. Since there seemed to be no other way, I got on

66

top of you and massaged your extremities until you went into something less like a coma and more like healthy sleep.'

'I can't remember any of that.' He giggled. 'It sounds rather fun. All my extremities?'

'It was not fun.'

Silence again. The turning came up and we began to climb quite steeply from the main road through pleasantly wooded hills.

'Archie?' he said at last.

'Yes?'

'I'm sorry.'

'OK.'

'Is it all right if I go back to sleep again?'

'Of course.'

'Right then. Archie?'

'Yes?'

'Easy on the bends, eh?'

We found a delightful spot – a camp-site just behind a very pleasant beach a mile or two east of the picturesque fishing-port of Ondárroa. Of course, there were disadvantages – early in the morning large sardine lorries thundered round the cliffs above our heads; the weather remained uncertain; at lunchtimes and at the weekend the beach became appallingly crowded: we were just about exactly half way between Bilbao and San Sebastián. But by and large we had a good time there. I particularly remember one lovely afternoon when the sun shone hotly, the tide was coming in over the rocks, and we searched for shrimps and gathered mussels ahead of it. That day Maurice was as happy – well – as happy as a sand boy. I like to think of him now – scrambling over the rocks, his skin just beginning to tan, his legs and arms smooth and wet from the spray; or crouching over a pool pushing his hair out of his eyes as he tried to manoeuvre a prawn into a cul-de-sac. He was thin but not skinny, fit but not athletic – in fact, very lovely.

How intent on everything and delighted with everything he was that day; the urge to fondle and kiss him was irresistible – I succumbed once and a lady nearby shepherded her children away, with many a backward look and dark Basque curses.

'Do it again,' Maurice crowed, 'go on, Archie, I dare you. Well, give us a kiss anyway.'

Then: 'Your heart's not in it this time.'

'Give over, Maurice, she'll have the guardias on us if we don't watch out.'

The day after that was not so good. The morning was cloudy and chilly again: it seemed an excursion was in order rather than a day by the beach. We went to Guernica. On the way we took in a cave system with some paintings in the first chambers. That was all right – I had never seen cave paintings before, they were good, but smaller than I had expected. But the rest became rather horrifying: there was about a mile more of caves, well-lit, with the usual stalactites and stalagmites, and the guide pointing out the formations that looked like elephant's ears, poached eggs, or boomed hollowly if you struck them. The trouble was that the path often ran along galleries quite high above the floor, and up and down long flights of iron ladders. There was absolutely no danger I am sure, but Maurice's vertigo struck again, and the rather claustrophobic atmosphere of the caves – no, claustrophobic is wrong, it is really fear of the unimaginable volumes above one – added to his state. There was no turning back; the regulations forbade the guide to leave us; naturally the other visitors, about twenty in all, did not want to miss some of what they had paid for. We just had to see it through, and Maurice hated it.

Guernica was depressing – perhaps because it was a dull day with low cloud – but one could not help associating the atmosphere with the history and noticing what one took to be signs of it. Although meticulously restored the buildings seemed new, unmellowed. One fancied the trees lining the streets and in the park were not as fully grown as they should have been. The bare square in front of the church was too reminiscent of the forty-year-old photograph one has seen, almost one hallucinates the bodies laid out in neat rows.

The famous oaks, both the old stump and the flourishing replacement under which the Kings of Spain bound themselves to respect Basque liberties and particular rights, seemed difficult to find, and difficult to get near: perhaps this is not acutally so, perhaps we just took a wrong turning or two. But on the whole I think this difficulty of access is intentional: the Tree is too much a symbol of the Basques' determination to return at least to the rights they had as recently as 1876, or even to the brief autonomy of 1936; too much a symbol of their determination to remain Basques to be left easily accessible either to a crowd or to a lone terrorist.

All in all a tiring and depressing day, made worse by generally execrable roads, and it put us in a bad temper with each other.

As we drove into Ondárroa I suggested stopping for a drink.

'Marvellous,' said Maurice, who had been on the wagon since the Eve of San Fermín, 'I'll have a Coke while you get boozed.'

'Don't be silly. You can have whatever you like.'

'Ta very nicely to the kind gentleman. But you'll bring your abacus to count how many I have.'

'Please don't be silly about it.'

'Please don't be silly about it,' he mimicked. 'Now I see it's all right after all for me to get alcoholic poisoning. What's so different today from four days ago . . . ' And so on, as I drove through the camp-site without stopping.

By the time we got there we were having a flaming

row which ended with me shouting: 'Please yourself. You stay here and open a tin of Heinz; I'm going back to Ondárroa to find the nicest fish restaurant I can. There's cream of chicken, tomato, or kidney. Have some of each, have a ball,' and off I went on foot.

It was about a mile and a half, up a steep hill, round the headland, down again to the village. At every step I expected to hear him coming up behind me, calling for me to wait, but he didn't.

I tried to get some pleasure out of seeing the boatyards where the high-prowed boats that fish the Bay of Biscay, the Bay of Basques, are still built; out of the harbour where the evening catch of sardines was being hoisted on to the quay to be packed away in crates between layers of ice from the ice factory across the way, but my heart wasn't really in it. On the phony Sunday Supplement principle of eating where the locals eat I chose the nearest place to the dock. The fish soup was too garlicky even for me, the spiced crab too expensive. The crew off the boat that had just come in ate pork chops which looked delicicous: they would, after spending a day working with fish. Then I walked back – feeling tired, fed up, apologetic, and a little fearful about what Maurice might have been up to in my absence.

I found him at the table in the van with the oil lamp lit in front of him, a bottle of brandy one third gone, and a strange man. For an angry moment I suspected another Norwegian style pick-up, but I was wrong.

CHAPTER 9

José Zumárraga is about forty-five and a typical Basque: that is to say he is shortish, squarely built, has a large round head set on a short neck above square powerful shoulders. His eyes are stony blue, his colouring fairer than most Spaniards, his mouth wide but thin-lipped. He was wearing an old dark suit, white shirt, no tie, a black beret. His hair is greyer than one expects, and he walks with a limp and the aid of thick, rubber-shod stick.

Maurice explained what had happened. It seems he had sulked for half an hour or so, expecting me to come back, but when I hadn't had thought that I might have got as far as the camp-site bar and stopped there to wait for him. Hoping to make amends therefore – this is his version – he had gone along expecting to find me there. He had a drink or two 'just sherry', and then realised that food was being served at a table under the window. 'Well, it wasn't tinned soup. It was mussels, and then grilled fresh sardines; it was jolly nice and all together cost a hundred and fifty pesetas with bread and wine.'

My own meal had cost three hundred and fifty, but I didn't say so.

'And I found I was sitting next to José here, and he was on his own too, so naturally we got talking – and he's still talking, telling me about his experiences with the Civil Guards and all the horrors he's been through. And now you can just sit quietly and let us get on with it.'

'I can speak English a little if you like,' said José.

'Not on your nelly,' cried Maurice. 'I'm here to listen to people speaking Spanish and to practise my own. Pay no attention to clammy knickers: I'll tell him everything tomorrow.'

71

José shrugged, held up the brandy bottle: I got myself a glass and told him to go ahead, both with the drink and his story. Really I had feared much worse from Maurice than the prospect of hearing him practise his Spanish for an hour or two late at night.

Next day and later he recounted José's story. This is what I remember of it.

José Zumárraga came from a bourgeois background, was well-educated, and in 1961 at the age of twenty-five entered a Basque law firm in Bilbao. From his earliest youth he had been a separatist. 'It was in my family, in my blood,' he said. His father, whom he had never known, had been assassinated in the pogrom following the Civil War, since when none of his relations had ever been able to get any sort of government post. 'Indeed, this is generally true: most posts more significant than railway porter go to Castilians,' he remarked. 'It is impossible for a Basque lawyer to be employed by a government agency if he remains in the País Vasco – if he goes to Andalusia, yes; if he remains at home, no. The same with teachers. One result of this is that there is a class of Castilian officials here who are virtually the bureaucracy of an occupying power. It is from this class that the right wing terrorists come, the Guerrilleros de Cristo Rey, for example.'

For some years he worked for the cause when he could in a fairly humble way – distributing leaflets, campaigning for the restoration of the Basque language and so on. At length the time came, inevitably, when the authorities decided that he had gone far enough. 'You do not have to be very important at all for this to happen. Perhaps I had simply upset some Castilian official, some member of the Cristo Rey movement, who knows? At all events I had sheltered none of the ETA, the Basque terrorists, whom I hate; planted no bombs; I have not been given secret military training. I had done nothing that would have been against the law in France or England, not even in Northern Ireland.'

Here Maurice had asked him why he was against the ETA.

'Not simply because they use terrorism, which I can understand as retaliation to terrorism from the other side, though I think it does more harm than good. No, but because the ETA is now divided into factions and all are revolutionaries. I am a separatist, a socialist, but a democrat too; not a Marxist-Leninist.'

One day he was returning from San Sebastián to Bilbao, on legal business, and was stopped at a road-block. The Guardias searched his car, found nothing, told him to drive on. Five kilometres later a second block stopped him.

'It was interesting, you see. Before I reached it the cars approaching me flashed their lights – so I knew there was a police trap ahead. But only ten minutes before I had been cleared, so I was sure I had nothing to fear.'

But this time the Guardias found pamphlets, apparently printed in Pau, in France, in the town where Maurice had been teaching. These urged the Basques to rise and massacre the duly constituted forces of law and order: the fact that these terms were actually used shows what a clumsy plant it was.

He was carried off immediately to prison in Zamora, two hundred miles to the south in the most pro-Franco area of Spain, and then to the notorious Carabanchel in Madrid. In both places he was lodged with murderers, rapists, hooligans who ingratiated themselves with the warders by beating up political prisoners. He was 'officially' beaten too, that is during interrogation, and suffered a form of water torture – his head being held down in buckets of filthy water. He was burned with cigarette ends.

At the partial amnesty declared when Juan Carlos acceded he was released since no connection with acts of

73

terrorism had been proved against him. 'I am lucky,' he said. 'I have friends who were there too and now they are *loco*, they are broken. Me, I am only *medio loco.*' He grinned, and helped himself to another finger of brandy.

The head of his law firm was sympathetic but unrelenting and would not give him back his job. 'The Cristo Rey said they would burn his offices if he did. Such threats should be believed.'

For the last six months he had picked up work where he could find it – labouring, shop assistant, giving private lessons.

At this point Maurice apparently asked him: 'Are you still active in the Separatist movement?'

José was silent for a moment, and then he pulled out a worn wallet and carefully took from it a neatly folded sheet of paper.

'This would be a good reason for not being so, don't you think?'

The document was so interesting to Maurice, as a piece for his collection of *realia*, that he copied it there and then. I have the copy in front of me now: with a dictionary and my memory of his translation I think I can put it into English. It was a letter.

Most Holy Society of Warriors of Christ the King
San Sebastián Branch

J.H.S.
San Sebastián, 4th May 1976
José Zumárraga, working in the area of Ondárroa

Dear Sir,
At a plenary meeting of this branch of our society on the fourth of this month we considered your recent conduct in and around Ondárroa. We believe, as a result of our investigations, that you are still in contact with members of the Communist

74

*Party, the Socialist Youth League, and the ETA,
all of whom in the past made daily threats on the life
of Francisco Franco, Caudillo of Spain and
Generalísimo of the Armed Forces, and now make
the same threats against the life of Juan Carlos, our
True King and Lord.*

*Such conduct on your part ill befits one of your
family, standing, and education; a graduate of the
Law School of Bilbao should at all times uphold the
Law.*

*We hereby give notice that unless you mend your
ways and renounce all contact with the above
traitors, we shall have no other remedy but to
GIVE YOU A LITTLE SHOT IN THE
BACK OF THE NECK.*

*This is the wish of our Society and of all good
patriots.*

*This was decided on the fourth of May, the first
year in the reign of His Majesty King Juan Carlos
I, Our Lord.*

Together we shout ¡Viva España! ¡Arriba
España! ¡Viva Francisco Franco! ¡Viva el Rey!

The signatures looked illegible though José insisted
that they could be easily identified, indeed were probably
very well known to the police.

This letter frightened me – still does.

'And it's not even true,' he added ruefully. 'I support
the National Basque Party. the PNV; I shall vote for a
socialist separatist when I get the chance – but I am not a
Marxist, I abhor them.'

'What did you do about it?' Maurice asked.

'I sent it to the local newspaper. The editor would have
liked to publish it but knew that at least his windows
would be broken if he did. Only a few weeks ago the
editor of a weekly supporting reforms was kidnapped in
Madrid, and taken into the Campo. There they slashed

75

his cheeks with razors and emptied a tin of red paint over him. They left him by the roadside forty miles from his home. The people who did this were proud to call themselves Warriors of Christ the King. So this was not published. I have also sent a copy to Juan Carlos – I thought he should know what is done in his name; but I have had no answer.'

In the chiaroscuro created by the lamplight, he looked like an apostle painted by Velásquez.

'But you asked me if I am still active and the answer is that in spite of everything, because of everything, for there is now nothing else to do, I am. And I break no laws. I support the PNV. Particularly I support Rafael Llodio – a fine man, a moderate, a man any Basque should be happy to vote for when democracy returns.'

'Tell Archie why you were eating in the camp-site restaurant tonight.'

José's expression darkened again and he continued, this time in his odd brand of American English.

'You know a woman was killed in Santurce today?'

'I don't even know where Santurce is.'

'It is on the coast, just the other side of Bilbao. Today was a holiday there, the Day of the Sardine. Many crowds go to see the blessing of the fishing-boats. Some men are carrying banners, asking for Basque independence, amnesty. The Guardias broke into the crowd to arrest them but they escaped, their banners furled, into a bar on the waterfront. It is not too clear what happened next. I believe some bar customers asked them in a sympathetic way what the banners said. My friends told these people. These people now produced pistols and tried to arrest my friends. My friends escaped into the road again but one of these people fired his pistol. His shots killed a woman who was passing.

'Now there is much trouble; there will be more demonstrations arising from this, perhaps more shooting. People will ask for the arrest of the *pistoleros*, but there will be no arrest. It will be like Montejurra again.'

'Montejurra?'

'Yes. It is where the Carlists, who are harmless cranks, hold their annual meeting in May. This year *pistoleros* turned up too, in coaches. Men were beaten, shot, at least one killed. There were pictures printed in the press, pictures of the *pistolero* with his gun in his hand, but still no arrest, no arrest even now.

'Today is the same. The killer was a Guardia in plain clothes or a member of the Cristo Rey as I believe; in either case such people are never arrested.

'As I say, today there is much trouble and when all the people together are angry, not just the activists who are always angry, then the Guardias try to find people like me, they rearrest us for questioning, lock us up for a day or two, rough us up a bit, and let us go when things have cooled. Partly this is so we will not organise, partly I think we are held as hostages. Anyway, at these times I come here, where I have a friend, and I stay for a few days. The Guardias do not look for me here amongst foreigners and Madrileños on holiday.' He drank again. 'That is why I am here. On account of this poor woman who is dead in Santurce.'

There was silence for a moment or two. The small windows in the side of the van were black except where they reflected the lamp or our faces: I felt vulnerable, the possibility that we could be seen by those we could not see. I could not help feeling that José might have chosen to be with us because he felt he was even safer in an English van than in a bar patronised by non-Basques.

He broke the silence, turned to Maurice and said: 'This Paco Blas you were telling me about earlier, the one you helped into Spain, you say you met him in Pau?'

'Yes, through some friends of mine.'

José turned his glass round slowly, eyeing the swing of the amber liquid.

'Well,' he went on, 'there are indeed many of our

77

people in Pau. In 1938, after the fascists had taken Irún and the Roncesvalles pass was closed, refugees went into Aragón and over Somport and Portalet. They came to Pau and went no further than they had to. I know many Spanish Basques in Pau. You must have been informed of our cause and in sympathy with it, to have helped this Paco.'

It was more a statement than a question; nevertheless, Maurice looked confused and wary too, and made no attempt to answer. Again I wondered just why he had helped Paco Blas.

A little later José went, perhaps politely aware that what he had told us had left us feeling uneasy. He said that there was a put-up cot waiting for him behind the bar which would now be closed.

After he had gone I went to the lavs. It was cold now with a bright starlit sky. I could hear the rumble of the Atlantic a quarter of a mile away, the chirp of a cricket nearer. Somewhere a dog barked. It was hard to believe that a woman, a harmless passer-by, a holiday-maker, had been absurdly shot dead that morning, only a few miles away. Again I shivered, as I had over José's letter from the Cristo Rey.

I understood quite clearly why Maurice had told José about the help we had given Paco Blas in the Pyrenees: clearly the boy's vanity had prompted that indiscretion – if indiscretion it was.

I smiled to myself as I returned to the van: really I could not disapprove too much of Maurice's vanity – for too long it had been the key back into his favour whenever we fell out with each other.

78

CHAPTER 10

Next day, Saturday, started fine and we were back down on the beach early. To begin with it was lovely – sunny, a stiff but warm breeze off the sea, surf with that lovely phenomenon surfers call 'glass' running along the top of each wave, yachts with spinnakers set towards San Sebastián, and La Grande Rhune thirty miles away in the French Pays Basque a lilac shadow on the horizon above St Jean de Luz and Biarritz. Wellington directed the Battle of the Nivelle from the top.

By eleven o'clock the place was impossible: it had become a dynamic model for the population explosion. On the one side the tide was coming in, inexorably narrowing what had been a wide sweep of white sand, almost a semi-circle, into a crescent nail-paring; on the other the large car-park between the sea and the camp-site continued to fill first with hundreds, then thousands of Seats, Renaults, Simcas and Citroëns.

It was also a living proof of what the Basque Country means to the rest of Spain: a heavily populated and extremely prosperous wealth-generating area involving most of the country's steel industry, much of its car production, fisheries, canneries, ship and boat-building, light engineering, food processing and who knows what else, all serviced by a skilled work force earning wages not far, if at all, behind those of similar workers in France, and at least equivalent to their English or Italian counterparts. Imagine what St Ives, say, would be like on a warm Saturday in July if it was only twenty miles from Birmingham and you will get an idea of what the beach at Ondárroa had become in a matter of two or three hours.

The Basques have several sports peculiar to themselves,

ranging from their own version of *pelota* or *chistera* to wood-chopping. On a beach, all between ten and thirty hit hard rubber balls about with no purpose other than keeping the ball in the air for as long as they can. They use wooden bats shaped like paddles. To the competition-oriented Anglo-Saxon it seems pretty pointless, though on a crowded beach it generates its own excitement.

Take any patch a hundred yards square and you will find thirty couples banging these balls about, one hundred infants planting *ikurrinas,* the Basque National Flag, on their sand pies, thirty adults with tubular frame chairs, parasols, bottles of wine, cans of beer, knives, forks, bottle openers and transistor radios playing Basque music. Across your chosen patch two pale, scrawny Englishmen will be picking their way. Needless to say, it is only the Englishmen who get hit by the hard rubber balls. In our particular case, Maurice. On the ear.

Back in the van for lunch he sat at the table sulkily turning over the pages of the glossy official programme of San Fermín 1976 while I attempted a *tortilla* or potato and onion omelette, Spanish style.

'We haven't seen the bulls run yet,' he murmured.

Then: 'There's Paco Alcalde, Manzanares, and Niño de la Capea on Monday.'

And: 'El Viti on Wednesday. You ought to see El Viti. I saw him in Salamanca two years ago. Really he's like God. God the Father. Yes – El Viti for God, if you ask me.'

Finally: 'Actually he's had a poor season so far, so he'll be really trying on Wednesday. El Viti, I mean, not God. Mind you, I don't think God the Father's really had his heart in it so far this summer, do you? I mean not unless he's West Indian, which of course he might be. What do you say, Archie?'

'OK. We'll leave tomorrow morning early. But you just jolly well behave yourself.'

'Archie, you're a hero. A sailor. Actually the best way

of turning a *tortilla* is to slide it on to a plate and . . . '

On the way back I followed the minor road again over the mountains, but even so we did not cut out the Guardia Civil road blocks. With José Zumárraga's stories in mind the bitter electric taste – of what? Adrenalin? – flooded the saliva of my mouth as soon as we saw them, two hundred yards away, at the bottom of a hill with a steep rise beyond them.

There were two dark green jeeps parked on the verge and a little cluster of the dark green uniforms and the shiny black hats in front. Even at that first sight one noticed the evil muzzles of their machine carbines slung from their shoulders. I slowed down, straightaway. If they asked me to stop, even at the last moment, I wanted to be able to do so so quickly that there would be no room at all for doubt about my intentions. In the last twelve months, as I write this, at least two foreign tourists have been shot dead for failing to understand the Guardia Civil's not always clear instructions.

The order this time was clear, a semaphore consisting of a white disc inside a red circle on the end of a baton held up firmly at one hundred yards.

'Oh Lord,' said Maurice, 'oh dear. We've done nothing wrong Archie, have we?'

'Only the obvious,' I replied. 'And they won't know about that unless the van's bugged.'

He giggled, but nervously: 'It's probably against the law here.'

'It is. I checked before I left.'

At first it appeared to be a document check, nothing more, though throughout the process they showed not one glimmer of pleasantness – not a smile, or a gesture that suggested we were members of the same race. One man, older than the others, with jowls marked with deep vertical lines, went through our passports page by page, then the green card insurance, and finally the registration

81

book. Wherever he could, he cross-checked with the car, with our faces, from one document to the next. The occasional question that he asked – where were we going? where had we come from? – came in Spanish and Maurice replied in Spanish. A younger man stood behind him all the time fingering the safety catch on his carbine. A third prowled round the outside of the van. Three more watched silently from a distance. The man with the semaphore waved a couple of Spanish cars through without stopping them – which raised my feelings of paranoia to panic level.

At last the older man handed everything back, and, still without a smile, said: '*Hoppeeeen*'.

'What does that mean?' I asked Maurice.

'I don't know. It's not Spanish.'

'*Hoppeeen*,' Hitler repeated. His frown deepened and he stood back from my door.

'Perhaps it's Basque for "drive on",' I suggested, and reached for the ignition.

'These are not Basques.'

Then, with a bang on the metal panelling behind my ear, the prowler shouted: '*Abra la puerta de detrás.*'

Maurice screamed: 'Stop.'

I hadn't started. But I nearly had.

Maurice, near hysteria, went on: 'He wants the back door open.'

I got out, went round the back with the keys, undid the double doors. My knees were shaking.

Their search was perfunctory, which was as well. Beneath the mattress we had a rather silly magazine which Maurice had stolen from Auguste in Pau. I am sure the Guardias would have judged it to be offensive. But then James Callaghan, the Archbishop of Canterbury and Mary Whitehouse would have done so too. However, whatever they were looking for was not there, indeed judging from the way they carried on, was much larger than a magazine.

At last the one with the jowls said: *'Muy bien. Pasen.'*

'Which means?'

'Drive on.'

'Sure?'

'Quite sure.'

'What was all that about?' Maurice asked, a moment or two later.

'How do I know? I suppose it's connected with that poor woman in Santurce. Perhaps there's been more trouble arising out of it.'

'You know what they were looking for, don't you?'

'No.'

'A body. A live body. They were looking to see if we had a hidden passenger. "Hoppeeen", I ask you. Do you realise we could have been shot to pieces just because a fool Guardia who knew I spoke Spanish wanted to show off what he thought was English . . . '

He went on in this way for some miles. Reaction, I suppose. I must say we had both had a bit of a fright.

Looking back on it all now, Maurice might have been right – right about the reason for their examination of the inside of the van. On the other hand there is another explanation. It's just possible the Guardias, these particular Guardias, were more interested in checking the van's *potential* for carrying a hidden passenger, rather than whether it actually was or not.

Our plan was to arrive in Pamplona at about half-past two, a time when we were most likely to find a parking place outside the bullring. But on this occasion traffic police with diversion notices directed us into a side road almost as soon as we had passed inside the eighteenth century fortifications. In this area the streets are laid out in a grid; I turned left, then right, then left again hoping thus to get to the bullring after all, but we found ourselves approaching three armoured lorries filled with riot police clutching shields, batons, and protected by visored

83

helmets. It was a one-way street, they were facing the same way as we were going, there seemed nothing to do but park.

'Aren't we getting out?' Maurice asked after a moment or two.

'No, I don't think so.'

'Why not?'

'I think we're safer in the van.'

'But we'll miss it.'

'Miss what?'

'Whatever it is. Oh come on, Archie, you know I'm meant to get the full Spanish experience if I can. Stukely said so.'

'If the full Spanish experience includes a rubber bullet up your backside or a clubbed head, I think it's something you can do without.'

'Archie, you are *crude*. Have you ever seen a rubber bullet?' and he began to let himself out.

'Maurice. Please do as I say. You promised to be good.'

Suddenly he grew angry: pale and his brown eyes glittered. With his knuckles whitening on the window sill – he was now on the pavement looking in – he hissed: 'Archie, for God's sake stop being a flaming nurse-maid. You're getting on my tits.' And he walked away, leather tassels swinging over his bum. There was nothing to do but lock up and follow.

I caught up with him just short of Avenida de Carlos III, the main thoroughfare linking the eighteenth century Plaza del Castillo to the left with the modern Plaza del General Mola to the right. We were perhaps a hundred yards from General Mola. The pavements of Carlos III were almost empty, there was no traffic, but people were leaning out of almost every window. The head of the procession, demonstration, was just about to pass us. As far as we could see it stretched right back to the Plaza del Castillo and must have involved many thousands of

84

people – perhaps thirty or forty thousand.

It was an exciting, even exhilarating experience. They moved forward in closed ranks, arms for the most part linked. Just behind the first files came the *Ikurrina*, a large flag – white, green and red, oddly like the Union Jack with a straight cross superimposed on a diagonal one; then a banner which read *Navarra por la Amnistía*. The people seemed to be of all ages and classes though there was a preponderance from the age group eighteen to thirty and many were in the red scarf and whites of San Fermín. They looked involved, alive, happy. When we arrived they were chanting rhythmically '*Amnistía, Libertad*', and '*Askatasuna, Askatasuna*', which is Basque for Liberty. Then, as if at a signal, they stopped, several thousand clenched fists rose in the air and they began to sing, in terrible unison, an anthem that sounded like nothing so much as 'Land of my Fathers' as sung at Cardiff Arms Park. Only one verse, then relentlessly they moved on again and the chant changed to '*Santurce hermanos no os olvidamos*' – 'Santurce – we, brothers, will not forget you', and '*Vosotros los Fascistas sois los terroristas*' – 'It is you, the Fascists, who are the terrorists.'

Now, above the heads of those near us we could see the flag and the banner at the front wheeling left and then right round the fountain in General Mola, bringing the front of the procession up to the palace of the civil governor, and at that moment we heard one single detonation, not awfully loud, but deep and percussive. A tiny wisp of blue smoke drifted across the banner – there was stillness for perhaps a tenth of a second.

Then the banners began to toss and twist as if suddenly caught in a gale force eddy of wind, there were more explosions, screams – some very shrill and touched with deep panic (after all, demonstrators have been shot dead often enough in Spain, as well as in South Africa and East Europe) – and in front of us the march faltered and the chant broke down into a frenetic babble of conflicting voices. For one terrible moment the demonstration, so completely a unity before, became a whirlpool of opposing forces, warring in itself, and then it broke, sweeping us away with it as if on a tide, down the side street up which we had come.

We allowed ourselves to be carried perhaps a hundred yards; then I realised that a gang of youths in front of us, members of the same *peña* I suppose, were showing signs of rallying, were trying to slow or halt the flood, were likely to trap us between them and the police. I caught Maurice's arm and dragged him down an alley and into a doorway. The flow of people down the street we had left swelled suddenly, the noise grew, there were three more detonations, and then we both caught the gas. As far as I know it was the first experience for both of us – certainly for me. It was most unpleasant. With eyes streaming, doubts in the mind as to whether it was simply tear gas or could it be C.S., we had to move. To go further up the alley was to head towards General Mola; the only way out was to follow the now thin trickle in front of us – at least it would lead us back towards the van. I grabbed Maurice's sleeve and yanked him out; together we rounded the corner and stepped straight into the path of the first file of the *Policía Armada* only ten yards away. I still retain a vision of a horror in an insect mask – two circular glass eyes above an articulated tubular proboscis, and wielding a heavy stick – and then I stumbled, still choking.

The beating was swift, perfunctory; the pain far more psychic than physical. No doubt I suffered more hurt in the playgrounds of my childhood: but at my age one does not expect to be beaten at all, however mildly, and certainly not in broad daylight, by a policeman, on one's hands and knees on the pavement. Even now as I write this three weeks later my sense of outrage is indescribable, my blood boils at the memory of it all – the first blow across my back, the second across my buttocks, and five seconds later a quite nasty kick in the thigh, the only one which left a bruise.

I lay still for a minute, my arms over my head, my knees drawn in foetally; then I felt a hand dragging at my shoulder.

'Come on Archie, come on. I say, Archie?'

Maurice was all right, untouched. As the police came up to him he had simply screamed out: '*Soy inglés, soy inglés* – I'm English', and they had rushed on past him.

On the way back to the van – he held my arm and I allowed myself to limp a little – I took him to task over what I still feel was unforgivable and puerile in his behaviour – namely, the idiocy of getting involved in other people's politics, not out of concern for the causes involved (as I have said Maurice was as apolitical as Julie Andrews or the Queen), not even out of curiosity or the desire for a thrill, but to get 'valid experience on which to base language work (projects and essays) next term'.

But he was unmoved, unhurt, and high on the excitement of it all.

'Oh, Stukely'll be tickled to death to know you were knocked about in the cause of the latest language teaching theory,' he exclaimed. 'Just wait till I tell him.'

I sanctioned him: 'I'll knock *you* about if you do.'

CHAPTER 11

That evening, outside the bullring, Maurice continued his hunt for *realia*. We joined the queues under the massive plane trees at about half-past six, just as the evening's *corrida* was starting, knowing that we would have to wait until eight-thirty before they started selling for the next day. Naturally he got into conversation with three of our neighbours. They were: a plump, energetic, smiling autodidact, a liberal; a one-legged cripple with short slicked grey hair and reptilian eyes; and a neatly dressed lady of a sort one finds surprisingly often in Spain – *petit bourgeois*, Catholic, conservative, but independent, forceful even, running her own little business, a shop perhaps or dress-making, a rather admirable down-to-earth sort of person who knows what the world is like and therefore chooses clearheadedly to maintain standards and to have values, not because she believes her particular standards and values are inherently good or just, but because without them there would be untidiness, mess, anarchy.

All were fifty – give or take five years.

The plump little man was rather splendid. He waved his arms about, spoke too fast so he sometimes frothed, listened brightly like a robin on a fence, and then was off again – a conversationalist. He did not, he said, belong to a political party, clandestine or otherwise, but, and he wasn't afraid of saying it, he hated religious and political intolerance and the censorship that went with it. Only recently had he been able to get hold of books, records, and so on, ones he had longed to have even in his youth . . .

What books? asked Maurice.

Oh, social novels like those of Zola and Blasco Ibáñez, philosophical like *Candide;* records of Victor Jara, Violeta Parra, they were wonderful, such honesty, such courage. The Church was much to blame, no, not so much now (as the lady bridled a little), no the Church now was a force for Liberalism, he recognised that, had not the Archbishop in Madrid preached sermons in favour of Amnesty and Reconciliation? But the Church in the past, that, we had to admit, was a different matter. And still – the matter of religious toleration: did we know only two religions were allowed in Spain? Two? Yes. It was not illegal to be a Jehovah's Witness. Why not? No one could say.

What did they think of the Demonstration?

It was marvellous, stupendous, a great day; yes, he had been in it, hadn't we all? The faces of the lady and the cripple lost expression. And weren't the police pigs? What brutality – children had had to be dragged into bars so as not to be trampled to death – yes, the lady had seen that too, from her balcony. And why? What for? Everyone wanted amnesty, reconciliation, everyone. So why not demonstrate for it?

Yes, demonstrate, all right, said the cripple. But he didn't hold with stoppages and strikes. No, not for any reason at all. Strikes were wrong. They would bring the country to ruin, to Communism. Workers should know their place.

But things must change, must go on, insisted our volatile liberal – we must welcome improvement, whatever difficulties come with it . . .

Improvement yes, cried the cripple, and stumped his crutch up and down with agitation, but every man should know his place, keep his station. That was obvious, everyone knew that.

But things have been bad, very bad, insisted the liberal – religious indoctrination, lack of education, hard working-conditions, all must change, would change.

Perhaps things had been bad for some people, the lady accepted – for many, for many people, the liberal asserted – but, she went on, she had never had to complain. Oh yes, she agreed (this time the liberal bridled), she might have been lucky and she knew things could get better for a lot of people, but there was no need to turn everything over, not everything. And the liberal nodded his head enthusiastically, so his cheeks wobbled – no, there was no need to change *everything*, he agreed, just the things that needed changing.

The cripple did not want change at all. People should be content with what they had – that's what *he* had always believed. Strikers and agitators were all scum, scum. And he spat.

Maurice rather naughtily restored harmony by asking what they thought of the foreigners who came to Pamplona for San Fermín.

Some were good, some were all right. There were too many. In the first days of the *feria* there was too much drunkenness and filth. The lady would not go out in the streets, well not in some streets, for the sights she saw. But the worst had gone now, been arrested or told to leave. The cripple muttered dourly that only those who could afford to live in hotels should be allowed. And why, asked the lady, and why do most of them come? Simply because some *yanqui* no one had ever heard of wrote a book about it. A long time ago. No one read the book nowadays, she doubted if even its title was remembered. But that's why they came.

Was that why we came? asked the liberal with a twinkle. No, no. Of course not. We came, Maurice said, because he was a student of Spanish, and I liked Spain. And after Pamplona we plan to go down the Camino de Santiago, to arrive for the Saint's Day. The liberal moved his head from side to side signifying a certain lack of enthusiasm for saints and Holy Years – but the lady was keen, envious: *Los Reyes* – the King and Queen – would

90

be in Santiago, her paper had confirmed it that morning. She would love to see Los Reyes – especially Queen Sofía, so beautiful, such *gracia*, like a madonna.

At the ticket window the lady and the liberal bought three tickets each. The cripple bought fifteen, and paid for them with thousand-peseta notes taken from a large roll. He left five hundred for the man behind the window. During the next two days we saw him several times, and later we learnt the black market mark-up was as much as one thousand per cent: for a five pound ticket a rich tourist in his hotel paid fifty. No one benefits from the trade except the touts who are probably organised, and the police: since the trade is illegal and open, they must have been getting a rake-off. The people who suffer most are ordinary Spanish working people who are unable to queue during working hours before the feria opens and who therefore have to rely for a cheap ticket on those held back for sale the evening before each fight – only to find that they are sold out because so many are bought in blocks by the touts.

Why record all this? Because somehow, somewhere, somebody who was interested in us, someone we never saw and whose identity we never discovered, found out through this conversation that we were going to Santiago, by the Camino. I discovered later that Maurice had mentioned our plans to one other person – José Zumárraga, on the Ondárroa camp-site, while I was supping off spiced crab. But it was not he who put a very different sort of person on our track.

The next three days were very jolly; the best of the trip, and with so much that was awful to come I don't see why I shouldn't allow myself the pleasure of living through them again.

Each morning began with the running of the bulls – and after all the inflated emotion various writers (you know who, and what's his name, and likewise, never mind) get out of it, it was a relief to find it a *fun* experience, even at half-past seven in the morning.

First there was a brass band, a really good brass band in blue blazers with a very slick, silver-haired conductor, who played everyone's favourites at least once and *Ramo-o-o-na . . . Pamplo-o-ona* three times, and marched out to a *paso doble* incorporating the cornet fanfares used as signals in the ring and which also gave opportunities for us all to go *riau*, *riau*, *riau*, hands in the air, wrists twisting.

At exactly eight o'clock the gate was opened and three minutes later the first of the runners came panting into the ring. Slowly the stream grew until there was a bottleneck which exploded like a wave from a burst dam spilling perhaps a thousand youths into the ring, and through the middle, straight through, without a glance to either side, came the bulls, already blown, probably terrified, right across the ring and out the gate the other side and into the pens. They had twelve hours in which to get their breath back. As I say, it was exciting, it was fun, and for the very few lads who dared to keep just in front of the bulls with only a rolled copy of the morning's *Diario de Navarra* to knock on the beast's nose if he got too near, it was dangerous – dangerous enough to bring a touch of *emoción* to the spectacle. But as far as I am concerned any dark mystery of brute creation, any mystical power of muscle and blood exists only in the minds of non-Iberian beholders.

Once that was over the crowd chanted *vaquilla, vaquilla,* and the *machos*, still with their rolled papers which they waved in unison, sat on the sand in front of the pens. At last the president, who was also the chief of the municipal police (little or nothing to do with the brutes in green or grey who broke up the demonstration), gave a signal and one or more young cows were let out. At first these were very lively indeed. Several boys were tossed (though, because the horns were blunted or padded,

92

never gored) and one youth with a bushy black beard and a T-shirt inscribed AMNISTIA contrived a couple of professional passes with a blanket and was much cheered. As soon as the cows, or calves, tired, the steers were brought out to lead them back. This happened four or five times; finally the chief of police (he looked like Lord Mountbatten some years ago – his blue uniform and white gloves had a faintly naval air) decided that that was enough for today and we all, perhaps twenty thousand of us, wandered in great good humour out into the freshly washed streets and squares, feeling the July sun already warm on our backs, for a breakfast of hot thick chocolate and *churros* in one of the cafés.

This, the chocolate and *churros*, might cost fifteen bob a person, especially in the Plaza del Castillo, but . . . well, it was San Fermín, and we were all, the locals included, paying the same prices.

During the rest of the morning there was always something going on – giants and big-heads patrolled the main streets, the latter chasing children and girls and hitting them with inflated bladders; groups of Basque bands – flutes and drums – with dancers like the ones we had seen in Biarritz, popped up everywhere; towards midday the *peña* bands reappeared, and as the bars began to fill *riau, riau, riau* echoed down the narrow alleys. Now, everywhere, there was the sound of at least one big bass drum going thump, thump, thump nearby, and usually two or three; and a *peña* band on top of one was deafening. At two, or a little after, peace returned; the streets emptied save for the odd drunk or a waiter sweeping out his bar; the refuse lorries, for the second time in twenty-four hours, and wine and beer trucks made the rounds. Time for a large lunch, a couple of coñacs, an hour or two in bed.

Then, in the evening, after the bullfight, we wandered the streets arm in arm (not in Spain, *en fiesta*, a sign of what is known here as *Los Gayes*) and enjoyed the *toro de fuego*, the bars, the fireworks, and the *música regional* in the Plaza del Castillo. Here, before the pop groups took over later, flute and drum bands played *jotas*, the dance from Navarre and Aragón that is now popular all over Spain, and a thousand informal 'eights' capered, arms in the air to the lively music; and what was really extraordinary to see was the way, at the end of each figure, every girl in the square would spin one way, then the other, skirts swirling out together in the lamplight. Such spontaneous unison seemed to me – sentimental liberal that I am who has lectured on the significance of dance in Shakespeare – a fine symbol of the hope of reconciliation in a country emerging from forty years of ruthless repression.

One evening, the next to last, we saw Monique and Lili, the girls from Pau, across a bar where the horse-shoe counter cut the drinking area in half. It was impossibly crowded, no hope of getting across to them, and anyway they were with two *peña* boys in white drill and red scarves, but Maurice managed to shout across to them in French: Yes, they were having a lovely time, it was their third day; yes, perhaps we would see them at the bull-run or the *corrida* the next day; and yes thank you they had somewhere to stay, they were with friends. Monique had rouged her cheeks, wore a black beret, and a San Fermín scarf. Lili for some reason sported a top-hat, too large for her; the rim rested on her ears and almost obscured her eyes. We did not see them again, not at Pamplona, not until we were on our way to Santiago.

The best day was the last. At five o'clock we set off for the town centre, in our pockets the bullfight tickets which we had queued for the evening before. (That time the crowd got angry with the touts; a *gris*, police of public order, was called in, our cripple swung away unmolested with his usual sheaf. And now, only now, do I recall that he asked us, almost as if checking, if we were leaving on Thursday, if we were taking the Camino de Santiago

94

through Logroño.) Already the streets were filling as the *peñas* congregated for the last time at their favoured bars. At half-past five they unfurled their banners, formed up behind their bands, and set off a hundred to two hundred strong, equipped with huge *bocadillos* of ham and *tortilla* and plastic buckets filled with *sangria*, for their last parade round the town and up into the bullring.

The banners were often amusing, even daring: one depicted top-hatted members of the *búnker*, government officials surviving from Franco's time, paying money into a Swiss bank; another showed an Infant Jesus wearing a San Fermín scarf – the caption said, 'Look at Baby Jesus, he's wearing a red scarf, like a good republican'.

The bullring filled quickly and early. One by one the *peñas* marched in, climbed out of the arena, and up into the sunny cheap section which is entirely sold out to them. Here they made a dense mass of white, broken only by two blocks, one of grey and one of black – clubs that wore Basque smocks. The giant hollow cylinder began to roar, almost vibrate to the noise; anticipation sharpened; ring attendants in red shirts and black trousers came out with sprinklers and rakes to lay the sand – miraculously it hadn't rained since Sunday – and then at exactly six twenty-five the confused babel of shouting, dancing, singing, *riau riau riau*-ing fell quiet for a breathless second; the *peñas* rose together, perhaps ten thousand of them, fists in the air, and again the Basque hymn *Euskal Gudari* rang out, the anthem we first heard at the demonstration, ending in wave after wave of cheering that drowned the sound of the hooped cornets and kettle drums that signalled the entry of the *Alguaciles* with their white panaches and curvetting horses.

As bullfight critics, the *peñas* of Pamplona are not generally noted for their discrimination. This is a mistake. Granted they thunderously cheer any matador who tries to enliven the proceedings with the more showy ornaments; granted they go ecstatic over unnecessary risk; and granted they abhor the fighter, however good, who kills on the shady side of the ring in front of the most expensive seats. But they do know a sham when they see one and will whistle and hoot him out of the ring and all the way back to Seville; and they also, and most greatly to their credit, recognise what is true and genuine.

Nearly twenty years ago they made up a chant which has since been adapted all over the country to fit any popular hero at any time – for footballers, tennis players, I've heard it sung at a wedding for the groom. Not all Spaniards know that it originated on the sunny terraces at Pamplona and that it was first sung for one man only.

In Spanish it goes:

¡El Viti! ¡El Viti! El Viti es cojonudo:
Como el Viti no hay ninguno.

El Viti is the greatest
There's no one like El Viti.

Not the greatest *copla* in the language – but the jingle they sing it to has something of the opening bars of 'see the Conquering Hero' and sung *con brío*, by thousands, for the man it was first invented for, it is quite powerfully affecting.

And they would not have sung it that night, not even for El Viti himself, if he had not deserved it.

Santiago Martin Sánchez – yes, Santiago – known as El Viti because he comes from Vitigudino near Salamanca, is pushing forty which is old for matador. In 1974 he went into semi-retirement to run his bull-ranch; in 1976 he came back to fight a full season: I don't know why – it is as likely that he returned because he felt or was persuaded he still had something to offer *Toreo*, as that he needed the money. He is lantern-faced, tall, lean, pale but not at all swarthy: very much a Castilian – there is

96

nothing of the gypsy or Andalusian about him. His style of bullfighting is the purest that has been seen for many decades: he never ornaments, he never cheats, he is never even showy. With an ordinary bull he can therefore be dull. With a bad bull – a coward or a weakling – he is far better than most because he is quick, skilful, decent. With a good bull – well, with a good bull – *Como El Viti no hay ninguno*.

He almost never smiles and so another title he has is *La Trista Figura* – borrowed from an older idealist who also refused to compromise. Because of his dignity, his poise, his authority, and the respect given to him by all other *toreros*, he is also known as *Su Majestad*.

On this occasion his suit was bright crimson – as royal a red as one could imagine – and gold.

His first bull was weak. By the *faena* it was too far gone, and he killed it quickly and cleanly.

His second bull was strong, and brave, but unpredictable: a lesser matador would have ruined him by tiring him, by over-dominating him, or even by exaggerating the danger to justify an early kill. But after some awkward moments El Viti achieved exactly the right level of *mando*; when the *faena* came the bull was fixed in the lure, and ready to charge again and again until he dropped; between them they thus achieved five minutes or more of perfection.

If the kill had been flawless – and the reason it wasn't was a combination of El Viti's integrity taken with a last second return to unpredictability on the part of the bull – if the kill had been perfect the *peñas* would have gone up to the Cathedral and brought him San Fermín himself, gold mitre, crozier, jewels and all. As it was he received – two ears, three red scarves tied lovingly round his neck by worshippers who eluded the police to get to him, a black Basque smock, two live sucking pigs, and all the more conventional offerings a successful matador gets on his lap of honour: flowers, wallets, handbags, boxes of chocolates, cigars, wineskins, hats, and so on. And above all the song:

¡El Viti! ¡El Viti! El Viti es cojonudo

and at last he smiled – he smiled quite a lot. Not many people see Santiago Martín from Vitigudino smile.

The other bulls, the other matadors were good, even very good but

Como El Viti no hay ninguno.

At the end, with dusk gathering, the *peñas* flooded down from the terraces and into the ring, formed behind their banners and their bands, and headed out through the big gate, club by club, for their last procession round the town. As each approached the exit the upflung hands twisted yet again three times: *riau*, *riau*, *riau*, and out they danced. The later ones carried large, lit candles.

As we left I noticed that Maurice's grin, the silly grin one can't help wearing after a perfect occasion, had taken on a level of smug inanity that had to be explained.

He tried, but spluttered, tried again. At last, with eyes beginning to water, he managed to articulate: 'I know it's silly. It's daft, it really is. Oh Archie, please forgive me . . . I just couldn't help thinking, when all the *peñas* were trying to get out of the ring at once, well, when there was a bit of a jam, and no one seemed to want to go first, I couldn't help thinking, I'm sorry, but it just came to me: *That's an awful lot of Basques in one exit.*'

PART THREE

Pilgrims' Way

CHAPTER 12

We left next day, late in the morning, after first going to the market for bull meat from the *corrida* and hard Pamplona sausage, and then to the post office. Maurice apparently felt a need to send a cheeky card to Stukely.

Again he made a rather campish fuss over the royal images, both of them together this time, on the stamps. 'You don't understand, Archie,' he exclaimed, when I looked bored, 'there's never been a proper *king* in my lifetime – King George the Good died before I was born,' which came as something of a shock to me: I didn't like to be reminded so vividly of the difference between our ages. 'I'm so thrilled we're going to see them in Santiago,' he went on.

Did he see them in the end? I don't know, but probably not.

Anyway, we were still only about ten miles from Pamplona when the urge to stop for some lunch became pressing. Climbing up a steep wooded hill out of the plain we came across a large gravelled layby planted with pines which looked a pleasant enough spot. Since we had been crawling behind an enormous grinding lorry for a mile or so it wasn't altogether a surprise that the radiator began to hiss and spit as soon as I turned off the engine. I opened the bonnet and left it to cool and got into the back to prepare a salad and slice the sausage. After a moment or two I heard voices.

A white Renault 12, with an L for León number plate, had pulled up a few yards away. There was a girl, quite pretty, sitting in the passenger seat. The driver was chatting with Maurice and looking into our engine. The raised bonnet had more or less hidden them from me.

Wiping my hands on a cloth I climbed out through the back door and walked round to join them.

The newcomer was tall, late twenties, rather smooth in expensive looking shirt and slacks. He looked fit, sleek, well-to-do, and now I was closer I could see his dolly girl matched.

'He's asking if we are having trouble with our radiator.' Maurice looked slightly worried, wary. I couldn't see why.

'Not very serious,' I said. 'I just haven't checked it for a few days: I expect it needs topping up. I'll know better when it's cool.'

The visitor looked at me out of serious dark eyes while Maurice translated – I felt oddly that I was being weighed up, judged. Then he smiled and gold flickered in the corner of his mouth.

They went on talking in Spanish. As far as I could gather it was the normal sort of chit-chat one expects when strangers on the same road start talking – where were we going? how long a holiday had we? and so on. I heard the words Santiago, and Nájera too. After a moment I excused myself and went back into the van. There I discovered that our supply of fresh water was low, and since there was a little fountain across the road – a spout splashing into a shallow trough – I took up an empty jerry can and strolled across to fill it.

It was warm and pleasant and peaceful, standing there. In the foreground the steady trickle of water into the can teased my ear, further off the casual flow of question and answer between Maurice and the stranger, and then the hum of a distant lorry, and a bird chattering in the pines above. I felt relaxed, happy, on holiday.

The jerry can, plastic, capacity ten litres, slipped a little in the trough as the flow of water altered its balance, and something moved beside it, on the slime that coated the brown stone.

A snake. Not suddenly, but smoothly it slipped up on

to and over the shallow lip; with the faintest hiss of scales on stones and pine-needles slid down and away, leaving a dark trail of water wetness in the dust. Not long – eighteen inches at most, thin, almost stringy, but with a flattened evil lozenge of a head disproportionately large to the rest. Undoubtedly a viper – *vipera aspis*.

I shivered, stared fixedly at the tree root over which it had disappeared, then looked carefully all over the rest of the area: bright green ferns, cress-like plants, moss near the water outlet; stones bright brown and smooth where the water trickled over them. A butterfly flew crookedly through the sunlight, a dragon fly with sapphire wings and jet body hovered, darted, hovered again. I picked up the can, checked the road, and walked back across to the layby.

As I came up behind the Renault, behind the girl, she leant forward as if suddenly aware of where I was, and tried to cover something that was sticking half out of the dashboard shelf in front of her. I'm sure I wouldn't have noticed it if she hadn't moved. What I saw was the butt of a revolver, in a holster, with straps. I suppose it was the sort that is worn under the armpit.

The stranger looked up, straight at me, and spoke directly to me. Maurice translated.

'He's wishing us luck with the radiator on our way to Nájera.'

'Nájera?'

'I told him that's where we're stopping tonight.'

'Right. *Gracias*. Is he off then?'

'I think so.'

'*Gracias. Adiós.*'

'*Adiós señores. Buen viaje.*' He raised a hand, flashed gold again, got in his car. He murmured to the girl, who also waved to us. The Renault swung round, with tyres crackling in the gravel and accelerated away down the road.

'He's going the way he came,' Maurice said.

'Has he? I didn't see him arrive.' I shivered again. We got in the van.

'He seemed to have a lot to say for himself,' I added as I slopped water over the lettuce in the sink.

'He had *nothing* to say for himself. He had a lot to ask.'

'Such as?'

'Oh, nothing very sinister. Where we've been, where we're going, how I came to speak Spanish so well, why we were on this road.'

'Why shouldn't we be on this road?'

'He said it was an unusual one for foreigners.'

'But it is the one marked as the Camino de Santiago.'

'Yes. I told him that. He seemed keen to know how far we'd get tonight. I told him Nájera.'

'Why?'

'It seems about the right distance. Looks interesting in the Guide. Has a camp-site. Does it matter?'

'Not at all – it'll do as well as anywhere else. We're in no hurry.'

And I went back to slicing tomatoes. I didn't tell him about the gun or the snake. I didn't tell him that my Spanish was by now good enough for me to be fairly sure that it was the stranger who had mentioned Nájera first, not Maurice – but then perhaps the subject had already come up before I joined them outside.

'Archie?'

'Yes?'

'Do you think he was some sort of policeman, secret police, checking us out?'

'Perhaps. Something of the sort, anyway.'

For the rest of the day Maurice was nervy, anxious, impatient. He gets moods – inexplicable or that he'd rather not explain: I've learnt to live with them. I was determined not to let this one spoil my enjoyment of the Camino.

I do not subscribe to the conspiracy theory of history; I am not more than normally liable to feelings of hidden persecution. But it still seems odd to me that we could not find the camp-site in Logroño, about twelve miles before Nájera. What happened was this: we stopped at Puente La Reina to see the splendid wooden image of Sant'Iago in the Church, and the eleventh century bridge (the Wife of Bath on her ambler stopped here for sure). I had said to Maurice we were in no hurry – we had nine days in which to cover the four hundred and fifty miles between us and Santiago – at five o'clock it seemed reasonable to stop at Logroño rather than push on to Nájera. The sky looked stormy again and I wanted to barbecue the steaks of *carne de toro*, not possible in rain or darkness. When I suggested stopping, Maurice was at first noncommittal, later was insistent that we should go on. I couldn't see any reason for doing so: the camping map, also provided by the Tourist Office, clearly indicated a camp-site at Logroño.

We could not find it. We saw no signs for one. People in the town, according to Maurice who got out to ask, did not know of one. At last I gave way and we drove on.

The road now crossed a highish plateau of red earth with large outcrops of red rock, flat-topped, and in the distance, as always in Spain, mountains. The soil looked poor, the land eroded, the main, often the only crop, vines. Very soon it seemed we had left the green richness of north Navarre and the Basque county. Cumulonimbus piled up huge palaces – purple, orange, gold, white in a tremendous arc across our path, and lightning crackled along the whole horizon. Far off at first, perhaps as much as twelve miles away, curtains of dense rain slid slowly but effortlessly across the plain between us and the mountains, and a premature dusk gathered over the road.

Suddenly the lightning struck much nearer than it had and the thunder banged brusquely above us. The rain swept in on us, huge drops that shattered or bounced whitely off the black tarmac, carved instant runnels in the soft heaped-up banks of red soil along the road-side.

'*This* is rather fine,' I commented. 'We've seen some good storms in the last fortnight, but this is something else again.'

Maurice did not answer. Glancing across at him I noticed that he was quite savagely chewing at his nails.

'Oh dear, you're not frightened are you?'

'No, of course not, silly. Yes, I suppose it is all a bit tremendous. But you know I'm not into the *Sturm und Drang* or *Donner und Blitzen* bit.'

The flip reply reassured me; but a moment or two later he was chewing again.

Most of Nájera, all the old part including the monastery, is on the western bank of the Rio Oja and nestles beneath a high red outcrop honey-combed with caves. The new part is on the eastern side and is thus the part reached first, coming from Logroño. It is at the foot of a hill, the road takes a sudden bend to the left as one approaches the bridge, a further left turn at the bridge takes one down the side of a long park spread out between apartments and the river, a park thinly planted with poplars and acacias. There are a bandstand, a drinking fountain or two and seats. At the end of this park is the camp-site – a delapidated place amongst poplars, set around and actually in what was once a small bullring. As we drove through this park towards the camp-site it dawned on me that some sort of gun-fight was in progress.

One does not know what to do in such circumstances. In the event, I decided against putting my foot down and racing on, and equally turned down the possibility of U-turning or backing out. It seemed best to stop.

The darkness was now almost complete, the rain torrential, hammering on the roof, the lightning and thunder frequent and close. It is not surprising therefore that I had not immediately identified the intermittent flashes a hundred yards or so further on and to the right, towards the river, as gun-shots; in fact I hardly registered them at all as I drove slowly on, leaning forward, peering through the half-moon the windscreen wiper sliced through the rain, anxious not to miss the next sign for the camp-site.

But an automatic rifle makes a lot of noise and fired from only ten yards away is inescapable – even in a thunderstorm at dusk. *Seemed best to stop*, I wrote above. That was a lie. My panic prompted two simultaneous decisions: to go on and to go back. The result, obviously, was a stalled engine.

The gun yammered away again – a noise like a huge, heavy tin rolling fast down a steep flight of stone steps – and this time I saw where it was: in front on the left, behind a tree, shooting *across* us towards the distant flashes I had noticed but not identified moments earlier. Feeling suddenly very sick, I realised that if I had gone on I should have driven straight into a cross-fire. And even as this thought became clear a figure detached itself from the tree and, bent double clutching his infernal gun – clear in the headlights – leapt across the space to the next tree, a tree nearer us.

'Get your head down,' I screamed at Maurice, who I now saw – and the sight seemed the final push down a vertiginous slope into a world of utter madness – was actually in the very act of yanking open his sliding door. As I screamed I was punching the starter – the warm engine fired immediately – we were still in gear and my foot was on the accelerator and we kangarooed forward about five yards with a jump that threw us both against our seat backs. Miraculously this time, I juggled out of a second stall and still kangarooing we bounded a further thirty feet or so down the road before getting properly under control. Moving far too fast we reached the camp-site entrance in a matter of seconds – a skid that sent up a sheet of water and brought our tail round about thirty degrees halted us with the red and white boom actually touching the top of the bonnet.

'Oh Jesus Christ, oh damn you,' Maurice wailed. 'What are we going to do now?'

I thought, but did not give myself time to say it: get out of here before someone who thinks we are a getaway car shoots us up. I leapt out, ran round the front and yanked open Maurice's door. He had huddled himself up, was white and shivering, hysterical, and for a moment would not move. Annoyance flooded over my own fear and I pulled his arm.

'Come on Maurice, don't be an idiot.' The words were mild enough, but I was half screaming, half shouting. Already I was drenched; through the roar of the rain and the thunder I felt sure I could hear gunshots in the darkness out of which we had come, and now, glancing back, could certainly see a powerful flash-light waving about over by the river; the rain driving across it turned its beam into grey silk shot with silver, and, I thought, it's definitely coming our way.

I pulled again.

'Oh, for Christ's sake. Jesus, I've got to get out of the seat-belt, haven't I?'

At last he was unclipped. As he came free he fell on me almost sending us both sprawling into the vast puddle we had halted in, but gripping each other clumsily we caught a sort of balance and threw ourselves splashing round the end of the boom and into the camp-site office.

A clerkly looking man with a thin grey beard looked up from the accounts he was checking. His eyes were almost invisible behind spectacles that flashed in the light from a dim, bare bulb.

'Passports?' he said. 'Or camping carnet?'

I had no intention of going back to the van.

Yet it seemed ridiculous to explain to him that there was shooting going on outside and so we just stood there helplessly for ten seconds or so dripping on to his floor.

His expression of polite enquiry contracted into doubt, then irritation.

'Passports or carnets?' he repeated. 'You must have one or the other.'

His English was accented but good. How did he know we were English? Probably he didn't, I thought then: certainly we were not Spanish and most foreigners know some English. In fact I'm pretty sure now he knew not only who we were, but had been expecting us at just that moment: he must have heard the shooting in spite of the thunder and the pounding rain, and it wasn't bothering him.

Maurice and I looked at each other; we edged back against the wall between door and window.

'Just a minute,' I offered. 'The rain is very heavy, you know.'

The clerk lifted his counter flap and came out towards us. I supposed then that he had it in mind to check the vehicle at the barrier to see if there was anyone else in it, indeed if we belonged to it at all, but at that moment there was a clatter of boots on the concrete sidewalk, clearly audible above the rain; the flashlight we had seen before swung briefly across the streaming window-pane, and three guardias stormed in.

The Guardia Civil is often described in the English press as a para-military police force. And 'para', the *Shorter Oxford* tells me, means 'by the side of ' and by extension 'amiss, faulty, disordered, improper, wrong' and so on, so I'm not just too sure what 'paramilitary' means. At that moment they seemed more military than police. They were wearing archaic helmets with a German look about them – so German indeed that one suspected that they were World War Two surplus – dark green anoraks over dark green battle-dress, calf-high black boots. The first flourished a heavy automatic pistol and the rubber-cased flashlight; the other two carried machine carbines. These last looked, to my uneducated

109

eye, a great deal more up to date than the helmets.

They pushed us about a bit, not much, enough to discourage disobedience, and one of them frisked us thoroughly. If he had not had garlic on his breath and if I had not been terrified, I might have found the experience ambivalent. I recalled Maurice's effort in Pamplona and tried '*Soy inglés*' two or three times, which finally, I thought, got through to the officer.

'*Pasaportes, pasaportes y papeles,*' he commanded.

Still feeling nervous, no – terrified, as above, but arguing to myself that the arrival of *las fuerzas del orden público* must mean that the shooting had stopped, I stepped back out into the still pouring rain, hurried round to the driver's door of the van, climbed in, and reached down between the seats to the place where we kept the document box, and as I did so received the worst fright I had had up to then.

My sense of smell is acute: I don't smoke, never have, but there was someone in the van who obviously did. He smelt wet and sweaty as well, and also of something else: it took a moment to place what. Fireworks and machine oil. For a second or two I was ready to kid myself that he had been and gone, was no longer there. Then he gave an audible sniff.

I grabbed the box – I had meant to sort out what was wanted – and scuttled back into the office.

The Guardia holstered his automatic, took the box from me, and began to go through it. One of the others continued to watch us both, with his finger on the trigger of his carbine; the third leant against the door jamb and peered out into the rain. At every moment I expected him to start blazing away at my van – for I felt sure the intruder would expect me to give him away and so would try to escape while he could. But nothing happened. As minutes ticked by I began to realise that it was possible, just, that the intruder would not be discovered, that we would be stuck with him. Common sense now suggested that I should speak up, now, while I could, before we were committed however briefly to shielding a fugitive. But I couldn't decide to, simply could not. In England, under similar circumstances, there would have been no doubt, no hesitation at all. If I had been poorly informed about Spain, or ostrich-blind, as the ordinary tourist anxious to get through a trouble-free holiday usually is, I should have spoken up. But – I had heard José Zumárraga's story, I had actually been beaten and kicked in the streets of Pamplona, I had heard and read too many stories about atrocities and terrorism from the Guardias and their bully-boys, and I hesitated.

Even hesitation can be, in itself, an act of commitment. And I suppose I made mine then.

The officer dropped our passports, insurance and the rest back in the box, looked up and grinned.

'O.K., *señores*, I am sorry if we have made you troubled,' he began and then went on in Spanish, which Maurice translated. 'There has been trouble tonight with two Basque terrorists who were trying to rob a bank in the old town. One we caught, the other is still missing, but no doubt we will catch him too. It is not important for you, please forget it and have a good trip. I hope the weather clears up for you.'

He saluted smartly and was gone, with his two men behind him.

The clerk pulled over the document box, fished out our passports, and began to fill in the registration form.

'How many?' he asked. 'Just two adults?'

I made my commitment irretrievable and nodded dumbly.

I said nothing to Maurice while the registration ritual was completed – how could I? The clerk spoke English. But Maurice still looked very shaken indeed. 'It's all gone wrong,' he muttered, 'it's all gone bloody wrong.'

Now I knew just how wrong things were but he didn't. From his angle only relief seemed appropriate.

'What's gone wrong?' I managed to ask.

'Oh everything. The holiday. The trip. Oh, don't mind me, Archie, I'll be all right soon. It's just all been a bit of a fright, that's all.'

I grimaced dourly. I felt sick and cold now at the thought of the intruder, of the fright Maurice still had coming.

'O.K.,' said the clerk, looking up at last. 'Sorry about the guardias. Find yourselves a parking place – we're not crowded, so go where you please.'

We got into the van – I at any rate with sweaty palms and pounding heart. I pressed the starter, flicked the headlights up.

'Maurice,' I said, 'don't fuss now, but I think we've got one of the Basques they were hunting in the back with us.'

'You're darn right,' said a voice from the dark behind. 'And allow me to say how very wonderful you two guys are. Truly wonderful.'

The deep voice, the careful spacing of the words were unmistakable, even after more than a fortnight – Paco Blas, last seen in the French Pyrenees.

CHAPTER 13

I drove down the gravelled paths, turned off as soon as I saw a gap between poplar saplings unoccupied by tents or caravans, and parked. Then I climbed into the back between the front seats and drew the curtains before asking Maurice to switch on the interior light. Finally I lit the oil lamp. I was aware that Paco was sitting on the edge of the single bunk; now I saw that he was clutching the short muzzle of a machine carbine which was upright between his knees. The knuckles of his left hand were bleeding; his mouth was bleeding too, his lips were puffy, as was his left eye.

'Well, you came along at just about the right time,' he drawled. And as he did so his eyelids flickered, the whites glowing behind them, and he began to keel over slowly away from me. Maurice, who was at that point following me through from the front seats, managed to catch him, and together we somehow got him horizontal on the bunk. The gun clattered noisily to the floor.

'He must be hurt,' said Maurice.

I resisted the temptation to be sarcastic, though the mixture of fear and anxiety was precipitating a sour lump of bad temper behind my eyes.

I made a perfunctory and unskilled examination and could find nothing more serious than the scrapes and bruises I had already noticed: though the left side of his trousers – heavy denims – were marked with ground-in mud as though he had taken a nasty fall, even been dragged. I supposed there might be something more serious underneath. Just as I was contemplating removing his trousers to see, he came round again.

He groaned, began to sit up, clutched the left side of his

113

head and sank back again. I had a closer look, found more mud, a nasty scrape in the roots of the thick coarse black hair, and a very large lump.

'He's had a nasty knock there,' I said. 'He's probably got concussion at least.'

'What do you mean "at least"?'

'Well, he could have a fracture, I suppose.'

Paco groaned again, opened his eyes, squinted as if the dull light was painful.

'Hell, my head,' he said.

'What are we going to do with him?'

'Get him to a doctor, I should think.'

'*Joder*, no. Friends, no doctor, please. Not here in Nájera anyway.'

'We can't just leave him here.'

I sat down on the upholstered bench by the table; after a moment Maurice sat on the other side. We both looked at the man on the bunk. Apart from denim trousers he was wearing heavy boots and a dark shiny leather jacket – the sort you often see on truck drivers. On the floor by the gun was a small webbing haversack. I leant forward, lifted it by its strap – it was heavier than I expected. I put it down and things in it clunked together metallically.

The rain drummed on the roof.

'Why not?' said Paco. 'Why not leave me here?'

'Where? In a hotel or something, do you mean?' I asked.

The black heavy brows came together, as if concentrating.

'Hell, no. I mean here in your van. Look, I'll be all right in a day or two. Nobody need see me, need they? If we get caught, say I threatened you, right?'

We let it rain for another half minute.

'I still think you ought to see a doctor.'

'Listen friend, let me know what's best for me, OK? Let me stay a night or two. Then take me some place else, along whatever route you're on, and drop me off when we're well clear of this place. That's all I ask.'

His eyes opened during this, found mine, held me with the serious but blank look I remembered from before, then returned to the low ceiling, the bottom of a cupboard above him.

'Well, we'll see,' I said at last. 'Leave it to the morning anyway and then decide.'

We left the bull's meat for the next day, warmed-up some soup and started a new bottle of Fundador brandy. At least Maurice and I did – remembering vaguely some rule about concussion I wouldn't let Paco have any. He took three Codeine though.

I hardly speculated at all about how he had got his injuries, just assumed that he had had a nasty fall somewhere during his escape from the guardias.

Going to bed was a problem. The bunk Paco was on was a spare – we used it as a day-bed or sofa. At night we normally took the leg off the table, unhooked it from the side, and let it drop into place between the two benches; with more cushions the dining area thus became a double bed – which we shared. With Paco in the van I felt a forgotten sense of reticence return. That night – indeed for the rest of the time Paco was with us – Maurice stayed in the big bed while I slept uncomfortably across the front seats, filling the gap between them with the last of the cushions.

Fear, worry, and brandy produced a paralysing exhaustion: I did not sleep well, but I could not make my brain work properly over the events of the day, of the past weeks, nor of course could I talk properly with Maurice. I was aware of questions unanswered, but I was not even certain what the questions were. Even now, here in the Hostal de España in Santiago, just over a fortnight later, I'm still guessing at some of the answers; then, in Nájera, I was quite unable to distinguish out of

115

all the many experiences, sights, conversations and so on that had taken place since meeting Maurice at Biarritz, most of which I haven't recorded, those which had anything to do with the plight we were in.

During the night Paco vomited, and continued to complain of severe headache; by the morning it seemed very clear to me that he must see a doctor, or that a doctor should be brought to him. When I put this to him, at about nine o'clock, he tried to argue, then went very pale and looked as if he might faint again. He also seemed to have difficulty focusing. Maurice suggested that we should move to another town first: for a moment I thought Paco was going to agree to this; then, as if suddenly remembering something, he announced that that was not on either. There would be road blocks, at least for a day or two, he said. We must stay put.

At last I announced that I was going into town to get a doctor, and there was nothing he could do to stop me.

He closed his eyes, and his brows again knitted with concentration.

'All right,' he said finally, 'but Maurice must go. After all, Archie, you don't speak Spanish so well. I think I know a doctor in Nájera who can be trusted. At least he is a Basque. Please give me paper and envelope and I will write a note asking him to come.'

He sat up and managed to write, but obviously found the task difficult. He was careful not to let us see what he was writing; he sealed the envelope, addressed it, and gave it to Maurice.

'Don't open it,' he instructed. 'Make sure it gets into Doctor Gómez's hands only.'

Maurice looked at the address.

'Plaza del Caudillo?' he asked. 'How do I find that?'

Paco let his head go back on the pillows again and shut his eyes. 'Cross the river by the foot bridge,' he said, 'go straight up the main street towards the monastery. You can't miss it.'

Maurice was gone a long time – two and a half hours. When I remarked on it, Paco said: 'Maybe the doctor's busy. He'll come when he can.' In the the meantime I pottered about: turned out the floor carpets to dry – it was a blustery morning after the storm, with patches of hot sunshine between high white clouds; attempted to pass the time of day with other campers – mostly Dutch or Spanish; got out the barbecue ready for when Maurice should get back; washed down the van. There was a scrape on Maurice's door: I like to be careful about things like that, so I got out the touch-up paint and filled it in. I supposed it had happened in the tight parking at Pamplona. though I was surprised I hadn't noticed it before. All the time the questions in my mind took shape, pushed themselves into an order of precedence.

It was nearly twelve when Doctor Gómez drove up in a large black Seat with Maurice beside him. He was a cheery sort of man – tubby, pink-faced. He had large plump hands with the finely scrubbed look that doctors' hands often have. He went over Paco very thoroughly – probed and pushed, shone a light in his eyes, took his blood pressure, hit his knee with a hammer, made him repeat the Spanish equivalent of 'She sells sea-shells on the sea-shore'. Finally he announced that our friend had a moderately severe concussion; he did not think there was a fracture. Normally he would take an X-ray, but under the circumstances felt he could risk a diagnosis without one. This was the only reference he made to our, or Paco's, situation. Paco, he continued, should stay where he was for three days at least; that is, the van and all of us should stay put. If there was any deterioration in Paco's condition, then Maurice knew where to find him. In the meantime, some pills and a light diet – 'You can make *tortilla*? *Bueno*' – would help recovery. No alcohol.

'You will be here to see our great yearly show,' he said as he left, 'the performance of *Los Anales de Nájera* in the monastery.'

117

Throughout the next three days our patient did indeed improve – his superficial bouncy manner, his irritating bonhomie returned. Maurice, however, became steadily more and more silent, depressed, nervous. He rarely met my gaze; if I offered any sign of tenderness or asked him what was the matter he shrugged me off petulantly – though more than once on such occasions his eyes filled with tears. Clearly he was overwrought.

The gun – I examined it when Paco went to the lav – was an American M14, 7.62mm, fully automatic rifle: at least that's what it said on the stock. Actually I had handled one once; during the last six months of my National Service in Korea, a period I try not to think about much.

The doubts in my mind began to centre themselves, like iron filings responding to the pull of magnets, round two nodal points. One – Maurice obviously knew more about what was going on than I did: how much more? How to get him to tell me? Two – the coincidence of running into Paco at Nájera, just at the moment when he was engaged in a running gun-fight with the Guardia Civil, was too great to stomach: how had he known that we, of all people in the world, would be where we were, at just that moment?

CHAPTER 14

'How to get Maurice to tell me?' The problem was not simply the inhibiting physical presence of Paco Blas – though that was bad enough, Maurice and I were hardly ever away from the van together during the next two days – no, the root of the trouble lay in the nature of my relationship with Maurice. The fact is that with all his charm, his cleverness, and talent for languages, he was a quite deeply disturbed person. He had never known his parents, but had been brought up by an elderly lady who claimed to be his aunt. He had been very fond of her. She had kept a sweet-shop and had died, rather hideously I believe, of cancer of the liver when Maurice was thirteen. There followed a rootless period in barren foster homes during which, in spite of academic success, he sank rather low.

When I first knew him he was taking drugs – not yet out of addiction, but already compulsively, and had made at least one suicide attempt.

I think, I am sure, I did him a lot of good, but it was not easy. The point is we were (I hope still are, if he survives) in love, and that is something we both valued very highly – it was the absolute foundation of what happened between us. What I am trying to say is this: it would have been easy to read our relationship as a case of 'you come to bed with me every now and then and let me have my evil way, and in return I'll give you a bit of a home, something to rely on, keep away all those really very evil and nasty things that were bothering you before I came along'. Such a relationship would have been, as Maurice himself once said, 'too sordid for words, let alone deeds'. The result is that the help I gave him, wanted to give him, had to be offered with infinite tact, had to come, to grow out of what was between us, could not be handed to him overtly. Not to labour the point – he would stop drugging, for example, when he no longer needed to, and possibly being with me helped to remove the need, but he would not stop because I told him to, or withheld something from him when he went back to it. The situation was not helped by the fact that I was, as they say, old enough to be his father.

The result of all this was that he was very quick indeed to resent any prying or interference into any sort of problem or mess he was getting himself into: by the time we had spent another day in Nájera I knew he was in a mess – all the signs were there – but I also knew that I would have to wait for him to tell me and he would tell me only when he had coped for himself and it was all over or when he was finally sure that it had got beyond his ability to deal with on his own. And so I waited.

As to how Paco Blas had known where we would be and when, it seemed to me for a long time that this might be very closely connected with Maurice's mess. I think I even got to the point of postulating some sort of hold – blackmail or threat on Paco's part – but then something happened that satisfied me that if that was the case, it wasn't the whole story, he had known where to find us by much simpler, less devious means.

On our third and last evening at Nájera Maurice and I went to see *Los Anales,* the show recommended by the doctor. This turned out to be a sort of pageant, *son et lumière,* slice of epic theatre, all mixed up together and offered in the courtyard of the restored monastery. In many ways it was appallingly bad. A local medieval poet, Berceo, was resurrected in a prologue and invited by the local king to tell us the history of the place and he did so in a succession of scenes that started with orgiastic rites performed by furry paleolithics, went quickly through the Roman Conquest, lingered over the lives of two local

120

saints with quite extraordinary miraculous powers, showed us some pilgrims going through like us to Santiago in all the appropriate gear, and ended with a long and tedious resumé of the infighting between the kings of Navarra, Aragón and Castille in the later middle ages. Yet the whole thing was done with great gusto and, as far as lights and sound went, a high standard of professionalism. The crowd, almost entirely Spanish and the place was packed, loved it – booing the Devil, cheering the saints, gasping with horror at the machiavellianism of the princes, and calling out to friends in the chorus line when things got at all tedious.

A little girl with her grandparents bobbed up and down in the row in front of us, and was a confounded nuisance until Maurice whispered some monstrous obscenity in her ear, at which she curled up on Grandad's knee, put her thumb in her mouth, and slept.

It was all rather jolly, and we enjoyed ourselves.

We came out into a small very crowded square decorated for *fiesta* in red and yellow flags, and with large portraits of Juan Carlos and Sofía everywhere. One of the flags, however, had a more permanent look about it – tatty and on a pole over a doorway with the motto beneath *Todo por la Patria* – the Guardia Civil. I noticed then that we were in the Plaza del Caudillo.

'I say, you didn't tell me your Doctor Gómez had his surgery next to the Civil Guard,' I commented. 'That must have been quite terrifying for you.'

'Yes,' Maurice replied, 'though not actually next door. The doctor was down that way,' and he gestured behind us.

We pushed on through the crowd and back to the footbridge. Here we stopped and watched the night black waters of the Oja swirling below us.

'We mustn't let this business with Paco get us down,' I suggested. 'Tomorrow we'll be off, and I suppose we'll be able to drop him somewhere as he said, and that'll be that. Meanwhile we're standing over the Río Oja and we haven't had any yet.'

'Any what, Archie?'

'Rioja, silly.'

'You're right. Let's be naughty. Let's go back to the restaurant by the camp-site, and let's have the lamb chops grilled over vine shoots they advertise and a bottle of the best Rioja with it, and let's not tell Paco about it at all.' He giggled and took my arm.

As I have said, the camp-site with its restaurant was a converted bullring and, though dilapidated, it had *ambiente*. Maurice's idea seemed a good one. But once we'd ordered I realised that although the prices were very reasonable I would not have enough cash to pay. I told Maurice that I'd have to go back to the van for a traveller's cheque.

'OK,' he said, 'but mind – you're not to tell Paco we're here, and he's not to ask himself along.'

The van was parked close to a lamp, like a street lamp, set amongst the poplars. As I approached it a figure in a dark suit and black beret moved away from it, saw me, hesitated, and then limped off briskly with the aid of a stick. Almost immediately he was in shadow, passing along the side of a vast Dutch caravan, but in the brief moment under the lamp I had known it was José Zumárraga.

I called out. 'José, *hola*. It's all right, it's me, Archie. Maurice's friend.'

He quickened his awkward progress away from me, I stepped out, cutting across to get in front of him. He stopped when I was still ten yards away, turned and faced me. Something in his normally wise, frank face, now lit by the next lamp, made me stop too.

'No,' he hissed, in a loud whisper, 'please keep back. Please do not say you have seen me. I must go now.'

He moved off again and slowly I made my way back to the van. As I did so I felt relieved: there were still contradictions in it all – for example the fact that Paco had been apparently involved in a minor act of terrorism and José had said he detested terrorism – but the fact that José and Paco were allies, allies in touch with each other, made it far easier to believe that we were doing the right thing in helping Paco.

Paco pretended to be asleep when I got back to the van – pretended, for surely he had just been in conference with his fellow separatist. I got the cheques and walked back to the restaurant and as I did more things fell into place. One should never feel surprised to discover the extent of one's credulity when one is asked to believe what one wants to believe. It seemed to me then that Paco had known where to find us because of José, because Maurice had told José we were going to Santiago after Pamplona; perhaps José had even asked him to be sure we should be at Nájera on that night, just in case Paco needed us. There was more to it than this I felt sure, but I reckoned I now had the framework of it clear in my mind.

And tomorrow we would be leaving Nájera, and dropping Paco off somewhere further west, and it would really be all over. An adventure, exciting in its way, even if it had been quite horrid at times. Apart from the actual danger I had been bothered by the moral side too: whatever José said, whatever Paco had said in Pau about being only a propagandist, Paco at least, with his gun and the rest, was some sort of terrorist, and that was something I had not liked to think of. But both sides used terrorism – and the wrong side used it gratuitously and under the protection of the police. If there was a right side out of the two I felt we had been on it: all in all it stood to our credit that we had not given Paco up.

CHAPTER 15

Next morning, things worked out just as well as I had hoped they would, in fact even better, for Paco left us much sooner than I had expected.

But all this was after a rather annoying start. We were parked between poplar saplings with, as I have said, a tall metal lamp set in a cement plinth about one and a half feet high just behind us and to the left. To get out I could choose to go forward on to the gravelled track or back; and because a large French family tent was pitched in front of us and one of the saplings made the turn awkward, I decided to back. The rear fender smashed into the concrete plinth. The damage was not serious, but would cost perhaps twenty pounds when we got back to England, and the silliness of it irritated me. What had caused the shunt was the fact that the left-hand wing mirror was out of alignment – and I knew I ought to have checked it before starting.

All the same I was soon feeling better. The weather was fine, a bit blustery still so not too hot in spite of the brilliant sun, and Paco quite soon improved my state of mind even more. Once we were over the river and out of Nájera, heading west and, I supposed, clear of any possible road blocks, I became aware that he was off the bunk and sitting at the reconstituted table behind me.

'Do you know where you want to be dropped?' I asked.

'Yes, friend, I think I do. Maurice, you have a map there in front of you.'

There was silence for a minute or two, then Paco's voice again.

'You know, friends, I recall over breakfast this morning a conversation about San Millán. He was in your play last night, am I right? And you said you'd like to see the twin monasteries of San Millán de la Cogolla. Well that will suit me fine. You just drive up there, do your tourist thing, and some way along you'll find me gone. First you'll see me, then you won't.'

And he returned to the bunk, leaving the map on the table.

It surprised me that he was prepared to be put down so soon: the San Millán monasteries were less than twenty miles from Nájera, but I was very relieved and not moved to question his decision.

However, Maurice too was surprised. 'I thought you'd want to go at least as far as Burgos,' he said.

'Why so?' The voice from the bunk was a shade hostile now.

'Oh I don't know. Get back on the main routes, both road and rail, for Basque land, I suppose.'

'Don't you worry too much about it,' came the voice again. 'I know what I'm doing. The country round these monasteries is rough – a good area to disappear in. And we're still nearer Bilbao here than we will be in Burgos or beyond.'

Which left me, not unreasonably I think, with the impression he was heading back to Bilbao, the industrial centre of the Basque country.

San Millán, Saint Aemiliano, was a sixth-century saint who converted Visigoths, lived to an enormous age, performed various miracles, saw the Devil off a few times, and generally seemed to be an attractive old codger. Rather uncharacteristically he reappeared with Sant'Iago in the tenth and eleventh centuries, flying over the Spanish armies during various of their battles with the Moors, and for this reason for a time achieved an equivalent rating with the Patron. His shrine is an attractive place and one can, if one likes, enter into pseudo-

125

academic argument with the pompous and inaccurately informed guide – he enjoys this – and in the car-park there is a fountain of sweet water.

It was while I was drinking from this that Maurice announced that Paco had gone. I straightened, looked out over sunlit trees to distant mountains, took in the swan-down whiteness of the few brisk clouds, and danced a step or three of pure joy. Maurice's face too split open into a grin broad and helpless enough to appear stupid.

'Well, that's that,' he said.

'Oh yes, indeed. That is that,' I cried.

It is difficult now to recapture the elation we felt. Atlas must have felt that way when Hercules took the sky off his shoulders.

'Now we can get on with having a lovely holiday,' I announced as we drove down the steep bendy road to the lower monastery. 'At any rate for just as long as you can manage to curb your penchant for helping lame dogs and wounded gangsters. By the way, I suppose your friend has taken his ironmongery with him?'

'Yes, he has,' Maurice replied, a shade petulantly. It was silly of me not to resist the temptation to tease him, especially when we were so happy.

I suppose the same sort of feeling prompted me to return to the subject late that evening: I just could not resist getting a little of my own back for all the worry, anxiety and fear I had suffered.

We had not in fact got much further that day. In the first place we arrived at the lower monastery too late to see it in the morning and had to wait until four o'clock – this gave us an opportunity to continue our private celebration in more intimate ways – then too the Camino continued to produce its own less transient delights. For instance at Santo Domingo de la Calzada there is the church where two cocks are kept alive over the tomb of the saint to commemorate another miracle: a

126

traveller had been murdered, like us a pilgrim; the accused looked likely to get off; the saint called upon two trussed, gutted, spitted and roasted cockerels to testify to the truth; the fowl came to life and roundly put the finger on the crook who was duly put to death. Two cocks are, to this day, kept alive in a glassed-in cage above the tomb as a perpetual though probably ineffectual threat against all who would prey off innocent travellers.

A few miles further on we pulled off the road, explored tracks through fields, and finally parked against a hedge which separated the cultivated land from common pasture on a knoll above us.

It was a lovely peaceful spot. I got out the barbecue and grilled pork chops; the evening was warm so we set up our chairs outside and after we'd eaten we opened a second bottle of Rioja, and watched the last glimmers of gold and turquoise fade from the west. Spain had double summer time that year and it was not properly dark till after ten.

And then I started in again on the poor boy.

At first it was a simple matter of reminiscing together about the recent horrific past from the blissful security of the rosy present. Then as the level in the second bottle fell I became first shrewish, then quarrelsome.

For a time we were at cross purposes – I assumed then, and on reflection next morning, because of alcohol; now I realise it must have been because poor Maurice simply did not know how much I knew, how much I had guessed. I suppose always in such circumstances the guilty person (and guilty is not really the right word) always assumes more knowledge on the part of the person he has offended than the party of the second part actually has.

'Look,' I remember saying, 'I have managed to put it together sufficiently to realise that Paco knew that we would be in Nájera when we were because you had told José Zumárraga in Ondárroa that we would be.'

'But Archie . . . '

'Just a minute. I realise this was probably a follow-up to you swanking that we had already smuggled Paco into Spain on behalf of the Basques. Well almost smuggled – I don't suppose you told José about your blessed vertigo . . . ?'

'Archie?'

'But what I still don't understand, and what I really think I'm entitled to know, is just why Paco can always rely on you – and therefore me – to do whatever he wants, your vertigo permitting.'

'Look Archie, drop it can't you? It's all over now – Paco's gone, it's finished, just drop it.'

'Oh sure, it's all over. But I still think I ought to know just what sort of a hold Paco has over you. It's not your enduring love of Basques; I mean you're not going to play Lord Byron for the Basque cause, are you? The first thing, almost, you said to me in Biarritz, when we were watching those dancers, was that you were fed up with Basques.'

At this point he became almost tearful – as much out of feeling teased and cornered than anything else, I should imagine.

'Archie,' he hiccupped, 'you're being an awful pig. You've guessed, and honestly I don't think it needed an Einstein to do it, that Paco can blackmail me. What he's got on me is pretty serious, or else I'd never do the sort of thing he's made me do. All this terrorism, politics, whatever it is, you know it's not my scene. You know a bit, just a little, of how terrified I was on that mountain, and was just as terrified as you – no, an awful lot more terrified – in Nájera. Well, what I'm trying to say is, isn't that enough? What good does it do now if I tell you what he had on me?'

I sat for a minute and listened to the blood roaring in my ears.

'Archie. Don't ask me to tell you. Please?'

'All right. No. It's just that I've had a scare and now I want to know why. But if you don't want to tell me, then that's all right, I suppose. Tell me some time though perhaps, eh?'

Another silence. I looked across the lamplight at him. His eyes looked bruised beneath the lids the way they did when he was very tired or harassed or upset.

'I might, Archie,' he said solemnly, 'I might. But honestly I doubt if I will.'

We drank a bit more, emptied the bottle. Not without difficulty, I stood up.

'Where are you going, Archie?'

'To get the Fundador.'

'I'd rather you didn't.'

'Oh hell.'

I sat down again.

'Sulky knickers,' he said.

I felt irritated. And then, for what reason I don't know, an odd memory came back to me.

'Just one thing though,' I resumed. 'Just one thing more. One thing you ought to know.'

'What?'

'Your Paco isn't a Basque at all.'

'What do you mean?'

'Well not according to Auguste. That night after our episode in the Pyrenees, when you had gone to sleep and I went out with the others, Auguste said Paco isn't a Basque at all.'

The light was very dim, Maurice almost on the edge of its area, but I think he was suddenly yet more tense, more screwed up, nearer still to the edge of hysteria.

'Auguste was a flaming idiot to say that,' he said. Then, 'Look Archie, please give it up now, please, please. You said earlier we can have a lovely holiday now, and we can too, but not if you go on nagging. All right?'

Not for the first time I was betrayed by convulsive tenderness and I gave in.

129

CHAPTER 16

Although the next two or three days were amongst the most pleasant of the trip, the existence of Paco was still kept in our minds – by what seemed to be odd coincidences, by nagging doubts that continued to trouble me when I had nothing else to think about, by real coincidence too – like meeting up with Monique and Lili in a village in the middle of the Castilian Campo. But first we ran into José Zumárraga again – this time in Burgos, lunch time, next day.

Bugos is an attractive and interesting town: I should have liked to have spent longer there. El Cid, the legendary hammer of the Moors, started his adventures having trouble with the local burghers – their descendants have made amends by raising an enormous but attractive bronze equestrian statue to him at the end of the bridge one crosses to get to the old town; Wellington failed to take the castle and as a result put his army in serious trouble – his only military failure; Franco made the town his headquarters for the last two years of the Civil War.

We parked in the little square outside the Cathedral – splendid from the outside, like Cologne, same architect – and did our historico-cultural-tourist bit round the interior. Disappointing – too dark and gloomy, too much recent religiosity, though we found a statue of a Bishop Maurice, which gave my companion harmless pleasure. When we came out José Zumárraga was again standing near the van, and this time he did not limp off.

'*Hola,*' he smiled as we came up, '*¿Qué tal?*'

'*Muy bien,*' said Maurice, and we shook hands – José's paw heavy, large, strong.

130

There was a moment of awkwardness ended of course by us all speaking at once. The Basque's idea was the right one – to celebrate the coincidence of our meeting, he suggested we should go to a nearby bar for a *tinto* or two.

He led us carefully past two or three posh-looking tourist traps – cafés with deeply cushioned chrome chairs and lots of heavy gilt and dark-stained oak – to an ordinary little bar a hundred metres away up a cobbled street. Since it was nearly one there were already eight or nine people in there; the pin-ball machines were jangling away, and the juke-box offered us an old Stones number 'Let's Spend the Night Together'.

'*Muy típico*,' commented Maurice, without approval. He would have preferred one of the plusher places.

We had small glasses of red wine, and mussels in their shells with peppery sauce and raw onion. José asked us politely about our trip, where we had been and so on. Maurice told him about El Viti at Pamplona and *Los Anales de Nájera*, and the awkward silence descended again.

José's large, wide, Basque face became expressionless. For a second he chewed on a toothpick, then spat it out, fixed my eyes, and spoke in English.

'You gave some help to your friend Paco Blas, there,' he said.

We nodded.

'Was he badly hurt?'

'Not very. Apart from bruises and a black eye he had concussion. But it got better.'

'And now he's no longer with you.'

We told him how we had dropped him, or rather how he had disappeared, at San Millán de la Cogolla.

'He was going to make his way to Bilbao,' Maurice offered.

José's eyes returned to his drink. He nodded to himself for a moment, then looked up with a slightly forced smile.

'And now you are enjoying Burgos?' he asked. 'And then you go on down the Camino – what, let me see, through León, Astorga, Ponferrada to Santiago? A good trip.'

He tried to sound interested in what we were up to, but his friendliness seemed forced: at least he was preoccupied, wanted to think of something else. He was relieved when I said we ought to be going, that we planned to eat a picnic lunch somewhere on the road.

As we drove out neither of us commented on the meeting. Neither of us accepted it as a coincidence, I think we both hoped that it was not ill-omened.

A short way out of Burgos there was another Guardia Civil road-block – this time they waved us through without stopping us; that is not to say they did not take down our number, or identify us.

We drove on through low hills above which kites floated and dropped, past sand-coloured villages with square castles and groves of poplars, and so, bit by bit, into the northern sector of the Campo, the great corn land of Old Castile. Here the wheat harvest was just coming to an end: we stopped once to brew up a cup of tea and could see, from where we were, and all operating together within half a mile of each other, a huge combine harvester of what I imagine must be one of the latest types, a tiny mule-drawn automatic reaper which flattened the corn with shaky lathes into swathes and pushed them over the cutting edge, and finally an old couple with sickles mowing in the postures of Brueghel or, for all I know, those of their bronze age ancestors.

From Fromista on we were looking for a place to camp – it was now gone seven – and hoping to find a spot before the next advertised camp-site at Carrión de los Condes. 'Carry on up the Peerage,' said Maurice. We came upon about the best spot we ever found, on the outskirts of a tiny village called Villalcázar de Sirga.

Just outside the village and set back from the road there

was the usual strip of common grassland beneath poplars, along the banks of an almost dried-up rivulet. The grass was fresh, though short-cropped, the poplar leaves whispered all evening and all night, flocks of finches and sparrows made spinning cat's cradles between the tree-trunks. The Campo – the endless undulating plain of stubble and ripe wheat – was separated from us by the village threshing ground; the last workers were just leaving it as we arrived: mules and oxen which had dragged heavy sledges shod with jagged flints round and round all day over the newly cut grain, separating the ears from the straw; women wrapped like Moors in shawls to keep out the dust, who had winnowed the loosened seed by endlessly pitchforking it into the air; a tractor and wagon that had brought in load after load of cut wheat. One or two waved at us in a friendly enough way as they went, but were no doubt too tired to come over. Soon the area was deserted – except for three black scarecrows set amongst the low conical piles of grain, chaff, and straw.

I drank gin and tonic, Maurice rum and Coke, and we watched the air change and glow, watched the trees and bushes take on a glaucous evening bloom, followed the ghostly wings of an owl rowing like a white ship with muffled oars between the tree-tops above our heads – well, drank more gin with tonic, more rum with Coke. Later, we told each other, would be soon enough to eat.

Then, just as the darkness really did seem to be closing in, when the scarecrows had become hard-edged silhouettes against a still luminous but violet sky, we heard voices – high, lively, girlish, and two extraordinary figures appeared crossing the narrow little bridge a couple of hundred yards behind us.

'Oh Lord,' said Maurice, 'I do believe it's Moni and Lili.'

They were dressed in: black felt hats with wide floppy brims fastened up at the front with huge, white cockle-shells that glowed in the dusk; check flannel shirts, like lumberjacks'; heavy denim shorts – long, almost to the knees, with shiny studs and more straps than seemed useful; woollen stockings and heavy walking boots. They had rucksacks on their backs, small tin flasks clipped to their belts, and they carried thin but strong staffs of hazel. They were singing a popular French nursery song – '*A la Pêche de Moules*', but when they saw us and knew us for sure they shouted '*Les Anglais, les Anglais,*' and switched to 'Ten Green Bottles'.

Already a little drunk I looked at the large lemon moon that had pulled itself unnoticed over the velvet horizon, and I announced: 'This will be a mad, mad night.'

It was.

Breathlessly they explained, exclaimed, in a mixture of French and English, shrugging off their loads, pouring themselves drinks, hopping in and out of the van like hungry sparrows, wielding the bread-knife, waving hunks of our bread, our cheese, our sausage:

'We've made auto-stop from Pamplona – in easy stages – Oh, the people we've met, you've no idea – but just now, a truck driver – *Le routier? Quel sa'type, mais oui!* (This last from Lili, eyes wide in mock horror, then her eyelashes dipping flirtingly) *tu n'en as pas idée* – we had to descend, it was necessary – *oui, c'est vrai, absolue-ment* – and in the village they told us, they told us we could make our camp here – they were very good, they promised we should not be disturbed – *mais on nous a dit qu'il y avait une camionette anglaise et* – and we thought, hoped it might be you, and it is so nice it is, what a coincidence, eh Lili? – *très, très agréable, trés agréable*, said Lili.

We got out cushions for them, wine, lit the lamp. Moni unlaced her boots, and invited Maurice to pull them off, then her woollen stockings, and she stretched like a cat, spreading her toes as a cat does her paws.

134

'*Ooof,*' she said. '*Maurice, encore du vin, s'il te plaît* – that is much better, much better now.'

It had been difficult, they said, very difficult. They were determined to stick to the Camino, not to take the easy way; but so much of it was down by-roads, like this one, and it was silly; nevertheless, however silly, they stuck to their principles, yes indeed. Two very nice Portuguese – ve-e-errry ni-i-ice, Lili put in throatily – had picked them up in a Mercedes – *oui, c'est vrai, un vrai Mercedès* – brand new – *oui, oh, c'était si chic, merveilleux* – so many luxuries – *beaucoup de trucs* – outside Burgos and, as a matter of principle, they had had to ask to be dropped in no time at all because the Camino was no more the *Route Nationale*.

So they had made bad time.

And how had we been since Pampelune? Had we made good progress, had fun? Had we seen Auguste and Jeanne-Marie? Always one kept an eye open for them, though this was not sensible already, because they would not arrive at Santiago until the twenty-third and today was only the eighteenth. No nineteenth? *C'est vrai? Le dix-huit? Mais non* . . . Anyway the plan was that they would meet Auguste and Jeanne-Marie in Santiago and then go on together to Lisbon.

By some sort of telepathy I understood that Maurice did not want me to mention our further adventures with Paco; but he amused them and me with his account of *Los Anales de Nájera*.

We drank more, the moon rose higher. Its light from an empty sky, on silvery poplar trees, on the short grass and bushes, on the scarecrows even, grew unbearably beautiful.

'We have a tent,' said Monique at last, with a note of *ennui* in her voice.

'Surely these gentlemen will not make us raise our tent,' said Lili, slowly and carefully.

With a lot of giggling, and bumping up against each

135

other we fixed up the large bed in the van for them. Maurice headed for the bunk, I for the front seats.

'Mais no-o-o-on,' cried Lili again, 'that is not friendly I think.'

So we all got in the big bed. There wasn't really enough room to make other than perfunctory gestures towards anything more than friendliness. Though what we managed I enjoyed. I may not be strictly conventional in my tastes but I am not, I hope, too bigoted either.

It was a lovely evening, a splendid night – but dawn brought Paco Blas back to mind, and in an odd way. It's a cliché I suppose to say that one's brain often works over problems, puzzles in an unconscious way – that must have happened with me.

Excess and age brought me awake earlier than anyone else. I staggered out into a pearly grey pre-dawn and found a tree a decent way off. As I came back I noticed the scratches on the passenger door of the van, and at that moment connected them for the first time with the wing mirror in front of them that had been knocked out of alignment. And I then remembered that Maurice's reaction to the gunfire had been to pull open that door.

At the time I had thought he was planning to jump and run for cover. But, when we reached the camp-site entrance his seat belt had still been fastened. Surely he would have unfastened it first, if it had been his intention to jump?

And so he had opened the door to let Paco in. Paco must have been grabbing for the door when I made my kangaroo jump forward. Probably it was the mirror that had hit him and given him concussion. Still he had managed to follow us and get in while we were in the office and before the guardias arrived.

In short, I realised that Maurice had known not just that Paco might be there, but exactly where he would be, and when, and under what circumstances.

I sat on the step at the back of the van for ten minutes pondering all this, watching the light grow and wisps of mist forming above the rushes in the river bed, and I decided to forget it all. Whatever it meant no longer mattered – Paco was gone.

As I got back into the van – three tousled heads black, chestnut, gold on the pillow – a thrush warbled an opening phrase for the dawn chorus.

CHAPTER 17

The next day and night continued mainly jolly. As can be imagined the girls and Maurice got up very slowly with endless yawning, groaning, four or five cups of coffee each, and then interminable washing, brushing, and combing. A large flock of sheep went by to graze on the stubble of the Campo; two savage but perfectly trained dogs raced up and down the line like traffic cops on motor bikes, tongues out, bellies to the ground, ready to snap the nose off any that strayed from the path into the uncut corn.

''*Dias*,' said the shepherd.

''*Dias*,' we chorused back.

'I should like,' I announced as he went out of hearing, 'to be a shepherd.'

For some reason the three of them looked at me and fell about laughing.

The labourers returned to the threshing ground, the tractors with carts moved off into the Campo, a mule-drawn reaper clanked and creaked past us. Before we left the first load was in, the staked oxen began their circling as surely fixed in their paths as the constellations in theirs and the flailing sledges rumbled over the grain; the swathed women tossed it in the air, dust rose, chaff drifted across towards us, it got much hotter, and all this before we were ready to go.

We stopped at Carrión de los Condes for supplies and looked for the churches indicated in the guides: one had its roof off, no admittance, restoration in progress. In the other a very weepy, very crowded funeral was taking place. Later we were allowed in and in the gloom found some nice examples of twelfth-century wood carving – a

Virgen del Camino and a Sant'Iago. The priest said to Maurice: 'We have lots more in the loft, but I'm afraid the people don't like them much. They prefer this sort of thing.' He indicated a Lourdes type Virgin – porcelain face, white and blue silk robes, chrome halo. 'I change the others round every now and then – what else can I do?'

Take us up to the loft, I thought – but he didn't.

We shopped in the Spar Supermarket – several processed foods with English brand names on the shelves but all made in Holland or West Germany, except Shippam's paste. Very popular in Spain. I don't particularly like the stuff myself but I come from Chichester and you can always tell the day of the week there down East Street, by the smell outside the factory. We needed a lot of things: four people eat and especially drink three times what two people do. Two girls, it seems, use eight times as much water as two men.

We had a long picnic and a longer siesta in another poplar grove out on the Campo: Moni read *Emma* in preparation for some exam or other I suppose, because, to my distress, she obviously hated it; in between answering her querulous questions on it I watched a pair of buzzards and later a marsh harrier scouting along the ditches between the fields; Maurice and Lili had a quietly giggly time behind an awning we had rigged up outside.

With the recent past still on my mind I asked Moni: 'Maurice had a bad spell earlier in the year, I think?'

'In Pau? Yes, he did.'

'Very bad?'

'Very serious.'

There was a pause and then very properly she went on: 'If he hasn't told you about it, I don't think I should, do you?'

And I left it at that.

At Sahagún Maurice bought the day's papers: 18TH JULY (read the headline in *Pueblo*) DAWN OF VIOLENCE – 28 BOMBS EXPLODED IN ALL MAJOR CITIES.

Bit by bit he picked it all out and pieced it together. The eighteenth had been the fortieth anniversary of the rising against the republican government, the beginning of the Civil War. On the one side the Fascist organisations celebrated masses and memorial services and re-asserted their faith in their recently deceased leader and his ideals; on the other, twenty-eight bombs went off simultaneously all over Spain. Since the explosions were at monuments to the Civil War dead (Franco's side only), or in government offices, and all took place in the very early hours, there were very few casualties. The only death was in Segovia where officers of the Guardia Civil fired on three youths who failed to stop when asked to. Two got away, the third was found and died later of gunshot wounds in hospital.

'*Mon Dieu*,' cried Lili, 'it was Saturday night, Sunday morning – they were on their way home from a *boum*.'

'It doesn't actually say so,' said Maurice.

'What about Bilbao?' I asked.

'Bilbao? Oh yes. Yes. I see what you mean.' He turned the pages. 'Ah yes. Here we are. Two bombs, around four in the morning. Both at headquarters of official, that is Falangist, unions. Lots of damage. No one hurt. One of the offices more or less completely smashed and rendered unusable. In the other, they reckon the bomb was planted by a man pretending to be a workman. Nothing much more.'

'Why the interest in Bilbao?' Moni asked.

'We suspect Paco Blas might have had something to do with it,' I said.

Immediately a chill silence fell over the three of them. Maurice went pale; Moni looked angry. Lili at last shrugged: '*Peut-être*,' she said, and went on in French, 'that dirty type would do anything if the price was right, even bomb Fascists.'

'Well,' I said, trying to move the conversation on from something that troubled them, I had no idea what, 'all that explains the road block outside Burgos yesterday. All this bombing and so on, I mean.'

Even so the mood remained sobered for some time, indeed almost until we camped again for the night. A few miles short of León, we turned left and drove a long way up the extraordinarily fertile *vega* of the Río Esla. Because it was so fertile we couldn't find a good camping place for miles – the fields were all intensely cultivated, or boggy and harbouring mosquitoes, or fenced off and filled with large udder-swinging cattle; and an awful lot of the road wasn't road at all but village high street: where in the Campo large villages occur every seven or eight miles, here small ones made an almost continuous ribbon. In the end we found a stubble field with only the minor inconvenience that we had to share it with a large Austrian family who arrived in a converted Volkswagen and pitched a tent as well.

The evening marked the second stage in intimate relationships however unconventional or even bizarre: after the somewhat bacchanalian excesses of the night before – the first stage – tranquil domesticity now set in. The girls quietly cooked a fairly authentic paella for us while on the front seats Maurice and I went through the other papers he had bought. Dimly I wondered how long it would be before third stage quarrels arising out of our mutual *ennui* would darken the horizon – one night? one week? I hoped we would be civilised about the break-up when it came.

I find I can read most Spanish papers quite easily: it pleased me to try with Maurice's help and it gave him the illusion he was teaching me Spanish and made him feel useful to me. Out of the many news items we glanced over three might be mentioned now: speculation as to whether Juan Carlos would announce a widening of the amnesty at Santiago on the Saint's Day or whether he would wait for the end of his Galician tour a week later at La Coruña; the civil governor at La Coruña had refused requests for permitted demonstrations for Galician autonomy, for amnesty, for legalisation of all political parties during the period of the King's tour; and leaders of the Galician Separatist party intended to host a conference on devolution at Santiago during the week following the twenty-fifth – separatists from Catalunia, from Andalusia, from the Canary Islands were expected. The Basques would be represented by Rafael Llodio, the moderate who was rallying support at the expense of the Marxist-dominated ETA.

The best paper of all, *El País*, had a leader condemning the bombs of the weekend; hoping for an end to all violence, it pointed out that such outrages could help only the extreme left and the extreme right, the tiny minorities who would lose all hope of seizing power once the nation had returned to democracy.

After the paella the atmosphere, while remaining domestic, became more excitable: Moni and Lili attempted to teach us *Belote*. I partnered Moni against the other two – Lili cheated outrageously and Maurice threatened to sulk; nevertheless, Moni and I won handsomely – twenty-five pesetas each. But what an absurd game it is where a jack sometimes counts as 20, sometimes 2, but never 10 or 11; where a 9 is sometimes 14, sometimes zero, but never 9.

CHAPTER 18

I have dwelt irrelevantly on the pleasures of those few hours between leaving Nájera and arriving in León because I look back on them with a nostalgia as painful if not as desperate as Adam must have experienced when contemplating Eden. The pain is a necessary concomitant of keeping the memory alive. Yet the rest of what happened will be more painful to tell and I must admit I have been putting off getting down to it.

A less hungover and earlier rising than that of the previous day allowed us to enter León, the third of the three major cities on the Camino, at about ten o'clock in the morning. The guide books indicated that visits to the Cathedral and to the Basilica of the College of San Isidoro were mandatory. But Maurice already knew León – he had attended a summer school there five years before, and Moni and Lili wanted to look at the market and the shops. We arranged that I should visit the Cathedral before meeting them at San Isidoro.

No doubt we were spotted and followed while we were still driving up the main road from the south-east, but of course I was not aware of this at the time.

I suppose too that I should be grateful that I was allowed to walk round the Cathedral unmolested. It has over two thousand square feet of mediaeval stained glass, the nave is clear for the most part so the patterns of coloured light are echoed dimly on the floor. Here and there tiny panes are missing and the sun throws through the gaps incandescent spots on the ends of pencil beams that swing with the rolling of the earth. One should no doubt explore this light-show for hours; lose oneself in the interplay between abstract pattern and the portrayal of myth, delve into the symbolism it all incorporates – obvious in its presence, but tantalisingly complex in its interlocking levels of neo-Aristotelianism and Christianity; no doubt. But as I returned to the west end, thinking to make a second and more considered circuit, Paco Blas plucked himself away from the base of a soaring column where he had been unrecognisable, almost hidden, and put himself right into my path, only five paces ahead of me. It would have been absurd to pretend that I had not seen him.

He was dressed as he had been when we last saw him – dark leather jacket, denims, black calf-length boots. Instead of a gun, he carried a cylindrical dark blue bag – like the kit bags soldiers on leave used to tote. His grin twisted up at me; his eyes, still bruised and swollen, held their usual iciness.

'Hi there, Mr Connaught. Isn't this just the greatest thing to bump into you here? Just like that?' and he snapped his fingers. Dumbly I moved on, levelled with him, hesitated, went on towards the door. He fell in beside me. His rubber-soled boots made no noise on the flags. 'I guess you've seen all you want to see in here,' he gestured vaguely. 'Pretty, don't you think? But not a lot to it. You know what I like in churches? I like a lot of gold, twirly pillars, cupids, and swags of fruits. What's that called? Baroque. That's it, Mr Connaught. They told me you were an educated man.'

I tripped on the low bar that ran across the threshold and he steadied my elbow. We stood in the square – hot, white light – and blinked.

'I think I'd like to buy you a drink, Mr Connaught. Just a way of saying thank you for the help you gave me in Nájera.'

He took me to a plush café – the sort we had avoided since Les Colonnes at Biarritz, and ordered German beers. They came quickly – tall bottles clad in silver foil with embossed labels, frosted with icy condensation.

The waiter poured; the bubbles floated up with the leisureliness one associates with the best. I hoped I would not be left with the bill.

He leant forward over the low, black-lacquered table and folded both hands round his . . . *stein*, I suppose is the right word. I took in the discolouration, blue shading to yellow, round his left eye, and wondered, not without malice, if it had indeed been my panic-struck kanga-rooing that had caused it.

'Archie – I can call you that? Right? I did before? OK. I just wasn't too sure how we were: I had begun to feel before I left that you were just a little tired of me – but it's still Archie and Paco? Fine. Just fine. Because I want you to take me from here, in your motorised caravan, to Santiago. How about that?'

I looked out of the huge plate glass window at the crowds hurrying up and down the boulevard outside. An immaculate traffic policeman in blue with a white solar topee, white gloves, and silver whistle, beckoned, halted, guided and occasionally chided the obedient mob around him. My feelings were mixed: on the one side a residue of the excitement and even the self-importance that went with helping Basque Separatists, on the other a determination not to be frightened silly again, not to have Maurice being upset in the obscure way Paco always achieved, not to have our holiday messed up. A previously unrealised personal distaste for Blas himself finally decided me.

'Señor Blas. I'll drink this beer with you, and then I'd like you to get out. I don't want to see you again.'

After I had said this my heart beat faster, anxiety welled up inside me, yet the flow over the crossing started, stopped, and started again before I dared to look back at him. When I did it was to find that he hadn't moved, his expression was the same – lop-sided grin, eyes bleak. But his shoulders now lifted in a tiny shrug as of resignation in the face of an unimportant though unpleasant task. Unhurriedly his hand went inside his leather jacket – absurdly I expected it to emerge clutching a huge automatic – and from a wallet he extracted a post-card sized photograph. He flipped it on the table and then leant back deeply in the soft leather cushions behind him. His grin broadened.

'Know him? I mean do you know that guy?'

I picked up the snap.

It was of a very attractive sixteen- or seventeen-year-old youth. He had long curly blond hair, a secret but charming smile, and he was holding up a *bota*, leather wine-bottle – not to drink out of it, but rather as if it was a fish he had just caught.

I must have shaken my head.

'No? I thought not. Well let me tell you a thing or two about that boy.' Suddenly, with a false drama that sickened me, he came forward again, as near to me as he could get, and spat out what he had to say in a clipped monotone, like a detective in a bad tele-series. 'Name: Jean Dupont; born 1959; father prominent shop-owner in Béarn; upper bourgeois, well-to-do, respectable; education: state lycée. Death: by suicide, under conditions not fully explained, by means of his father's hunting gun. Blew his brains out.'

He drank some beer.

'Right. You can read that much in *La République des Pyrénées*, edition of 15th November, 1975. The police know a little more: he was high on acid when he did it. A bad trip – you've read of them, even if you've never had one. What the French police don't know, what his father suspects, and what I can prove – is this. He got the acid, and the habit of dropping it, from the English *assistant* at that Lycée, with whom he had a homosexual relationship. I guess you know who that English *assistant* is – but man, I can prove it. If the French police get my proof, they'll put him away for several years – and, yeah, you know it, there's easy extradition between France and

146

England. On the other hand if I put it in Monsieur Dupont's way, he'll blow your fancy boy's brains out. He was very fond of his son. Right?'

Slowly, wishing with every syllable I could reach across the table and hammer him into a bleeding mess, I explained to him that Moni and Lili were with us. He frowned, thought for a moment or two, then shrugged again. 'OK. So you'll have to get rid of them, that's all. But friend, don't tell them why. It'll be a whole lot better if you don't mention me. All right? I want you to remember that. Get them out by – let's see; hell, I'm in no hurry, by nightfall. Park by the bullring, I'll find you there. Great. I'll be along an hour after dusk. Say ten-thirty. By then be sure the girls are gone. Just you and Maurice, there. OK?'

He finished his beer, put down a hundred peseta note, picked up the photo, his kit bag, grinned at me and was gone.

I followed, unsteadily, out into the noisy street. I suppose the hundred pesetas was enough; anyway no one challenged me for more. My glass remained untouched.

CHAPTER 19

There was still half an hour to waste before I was due to meet Maurice and the girls, but I could think of no way of passing it other than to go to San Isidoro and wait for them there. I found a small modern square just in sight of the college entrance and began to walk manically round it, no doubt fidgeting, checking my watch, generally looking disturbed: I became conscious that I was attracting anxious glances from strangers and I forced myself to sit down on a simple granite bench. Almost as soon as I had, I noticed a square dark figure, black beret and rubber-tipped walking stick, moving from the far corner across the hot paving stones towards me. Dumbly conscious that anxiety had tightened an unbelievable further turn on my insides, I stayed put until José Zumárraga sat down beside me.

'I should have preferred a less conspicuous place,' he said. 'However, I am not known here, I think, so we can talk briefly.'

There was nothing I could say, so I waited.

'Paco Blas has spoken to you, then?'

I nodded.

'I witnessed your meeting in the cathedral.'

The rubber ferrule prodded at a gum-wrapper near my foot.

'You have agreed to take him to Santiago de Compostela?'

'Against my will, yes.'

'Of course against your will. You are not after all too concerned with our politics. But you will arrive when? On the twenty-fourth or before?'

'I don't know. I suppose with hard driving we could be

148

there tomorrow. Maurice and I had planned to travel slowly and arrive on the twenty-third or twenty-fourth.'

'But now of course you are not sure. It must be that you are waiting for Paco to tell you.'

Perhaps I shrugged.

'You will have to drop the girls who are with you.'

'Apparently. He said as much.'

'Good.' He stood up and held out his hand. Without knowing quite why, I took it and returned his grip. 'Thank you, Mr Connaught. You are being most helpful.'

With bewilderment now as well as anxiety I watched him stump his way down the side of the square, across the road, and then he was gone in the darkness of the side-street.

Since Paco had left me ten hours in which to get rid of Moni and Lili I decided to say nothing at all about meeting him again until we had finished with San Isidoro, but my appearance betrayed me. Not at first: when they arrived they all three were so concerned to tell me what they had seen, what they had bought – local food mostly; and then were so put out to find at the entrance (which was more like a cinema foyer than a monastery) that because the college was private, unsupported by state funds, their student cards earned no reduction, and the entrance fee was a hundred pesetas, that I don't think they would have noticed if I had turned green.

A spruce female guide dressed like an air-hostess in navy and white pushed us into a flock of about twenty other people and poured us all into the Royal Pantheon of the Ancient Kings of León like sheep into a pen. This Pantheon was a low ceilinged vaulted chapel with rows of dull looking tombs – not much till you looked up and found yourself gazing at the most perfectly preserved twelfth-century painting I have ever seen. Beneath an arch decorated with medallions depicting the twelve months of the year – each identified by some peasant

149

pursuit such as flailing wheat, killing a pig and so on – Maurice pulled my sleeve.

'You look as if you have seen a ghost.'

'I've seen Paco Blas.'

I thought he was going to faint.

'Oh hell. Oh damn, oh hell.'

The air-hostess, sheep-dog bitch, whatever she was, invited us to admire the portrayal of the angels' message to the shepherds – apparently she found humour in the characterisation of the peasants; however, the artist confined himself to solemn devotion in the next half-vault – the Nativity. Or so she said.

'We've got to take him to Santiago.'

'Got to?'

'Got to.'

People began to leak away out of a further door into a sunlit cloister. With his eyes still fixed on the ceiling – the Flight into Egypt this time – Maurice said: 'He must have told you about Jean Dupont.'

'Yes.'

The air-hostess coughed, not too discreetly. We were the only ones left. I took Maurice's elbow and pushed him towards her. As we passed into the cloister, she snapped off the light in the chapel, and then locked the door. On clacking heels she trotted up to the front of the group and headed them off into a hall. Dully we followed. It was an exhibition of photographs of the Pilgrims' Way.

'I don't want to see this,' said Maurice. 'Let's stay in the sun. Poor Jean. It wasn't my fault, whatever Paco told you. Poor Jean.'

He blinked, wiped his eyes on his sleeve. It's dreadful to admit that I felt embarrassed, hoped no one would notice. Only the guide was looking at us, wary that we didn't shoot off into some forbidden area. Moni and Lili were gossiping brightly over pictures of places they had seen.

'But you did give him LSD, and you did go to bed with him?' I asked.

'Yes.'

'And Paco can prove it?'

'Yes, if he says so. But he doesn't have to prove it. He's got circumstantial evidence. Enough for the French police to arrest me. Then they'll just keep on at me until I confess to anything they want. It's the way they work there.'

'Enough evidence to convince this Jean Dupont's father that he should kill you?'

'Is that what he said? Yes. And he would too. Monsieur Dupont, I mean.'

'So we take Paco Blas to Santiago.'

'Yes. Oh Archie, I'm so sorry I've dragged you into all this, you don't know how sorry.'

The party began to push back past us, through yet another door, up a flight of stairs. The guide announced that we were going to the Treasury. Moni and Lili came past.

'What's the matter with you two?' Moni asked.

'It's all right.'

'Are you sure? You both look dreadful.'

'Tell you later.'

'OK.'

Lili pulled one of those French faces – shoulders hunched, corners of the mouth pulled down, and they went on. Dutifully we followed, the last of all. The guide was tapping her foot at the top of the stairs, almost pushed us into another gallery, and locked the door behind us before surging into the middle of the group again. We were now, she told us, standing in the middle of what was perhaps the most priceless collection of mediaeval *objets d'art* in Spain.

'What about them?' Maurice indicated the girls. 'Does he know we've got them?'

'I told him. He said we must get rid of them.'

151

I turned away to a glass case, and found I was looking at a perfect ivory of the Crucifixion. It was mounted in gold. It did indeed look very valuable, I thought. I told Maurice that Paco would join us outside the bullring at half-past ten.

We had left the van in a side street not far from the Cathedral. We walked back to it – the girls in front still carrying their shopping, Maurice and I behind; the girls chattered, mostly, as far as I could gather, about the awfulness of the guide, of the awfulness of being chiv-vied round without being given a chance to look at things properly. They turned and faced us at the van, waiting for me to unlock the door.

'What is for the dinner?' Lili asked carefully. Then she giggled, and answered herself. 'We have the smelly cheese of León.'

'I'm sorry,' said Maurice. 'But you've got to go. Both of you.'

Moni looked, for a moment, as if she had been slapped. Then the colour rose angrily in her cheeks.

'It's because of Paco Blas,' Maurice hurried on, before I could stop him. 'He's found us here and he is making Archie and me take him to Santiago.'

We looked at each other in silence and the light and heat beat up at us off the scorching pavement.

'Very well,' said Moni, at last. 'Very well. Open the van and let us get our things.'

I did so.

Lili looked bewildered. *'Qu'est-ce qui se passe?'* she asked as she followed Moni in.

Maurice and I waited on the pavement.

'Oh non. C'est qu'ils sont des pédés, n'est-ce pas?' came Lili's voice.

Maurice almost smiled. *'Pédé* equals gay,' he murmured. Then he went on: 'Monique knows all about it. About Jean and me, and about Paco. She saved me in

152

November. Anyway she understands.'

'Paco said that I was not to tell Moni and Lili that it was because of him they had to leave. He was very emphatic about that.'

'You never said. Oh well. *Tant pis.*'

The girls came out again. There on the pavement Lili insisted on kissing us both passionately – with missionary zeal, I suspect. Then they were gone – black felt hats with scallop shells, rucksacks, hazel sticks, two round pert bottoms in denim shorts.

CHAPTER 20

We drove straight down to the bullring and sat out the
next ten hours waiting for Paco. There did not seem to be
anything else to do. We talked desultorily about it all, but
awkwardly, almost as if it was tiring to do so, a bore.
Maurice told me more about this Jean Dupont – from
what he said the fault had been far from exclusively his:
Jean had been in with an ugly crowd, smoked pot, was
into the milder hallucinogens. Maurice himself had
already been driven first to distraction and then back to
drug abuse by the noise of the lorries beneath his studio
window. They had grown fond of each other, though the
sex, he said, had been little more than a gesture. I told
him about the photo Paco had shown me. Maurice explained that it had been taken during a day-trip to Jaca the
previous October. Four of them had gone. One of the
others was from a family of Spanish exiles – he had taken
the pictures; a second picture had been of Maurice and
Jean fondling each other and kissing with put-on passion – 'silly stuff, childish, just a joke' – and this was
Paco's main weapon. It would certainly be enough to
bring the *flics* down on him again, or, for that matter,
make Monsieur Dupont reach for his shot-gun.

'Monsieur Dupont is a Gaullist Catholic, a wealthy
draper, and he hates me already without knowing quite
why.'

'How did Paco get hold of this photo?'

'I told you, the boy who took it has Spanish parents,
though he himself has a French passport. The exiles stick
together. Paco got to know them well as soon as he
arrived.'

'When was that?'

'I'm not too sure. The end of November, early December I think. Not long after Franco died.'

'After this Dupont business?'

'I think so. But of course the stink was still very much in the air. As I say, Paco got into our set through the Spaniards we knew; although he was older than most of us, he's got a sort of charm when he wants, and he had a lot of money to splash about. I didn't know of course but obviously he was worming things out about us, and eventually he got the photos – probably bought them with drugs, and a statement from the same boy saying he knew I'd given Jean the acid. Then a couple of months ago he asked me to find a way of smuggling him into Spain.'

'And you wrote to me.'

'Yes. But Archie, I was going to anyway. I truly wanted to come on this trip with you.'

Although we were in the shade, the afternoon got very hot. We opened all the windows, and sat in the van, at the table, trying to read; we even played a couple of games of backgammon. After a time, I became conscious of an awful smell – rotten cabbage, old clothes, Gorgonzola all mixed up. We had to hunt to find the source – a leaky packet left under the pillow in the bunk.

'Oh God,' cried Maurice, 'it's that foul cheese Lili bought.'

'What is it?'

'*Queso de Cabrales*. Local stuff. The strongest in the world.'

'I'll say.'

'They must have put it there for Paco to lie on. Archie,' he pleaded, 'let's put it back there.'

I unwrapped it: an orangy-brown slab with a texture like wet crumble, wrapped in chestnut leaves. I tried a bit on my finger – not as bad as it smelled.

'No. If it stays, and it'll have to behave if it wants to, it goes in a tupperware and in the cold box.'

As Maurice put it away, I asked: 'Just what has Moni got against Paco?'

'Well, she knows he's blackmailing me. But as well, I think Auguste told her something odd or bad about him. But I've never discovered just what.'

Later we cleaned out the van; I did some shopping between five and six; and questions went on nagging at me. At about eight, with the heat at last going off, we were sitting again at the table, this time with beers.

'What is Paco up to?' I asked.

Maurice almost flinched away. 'I don't know. How should I know? He's some sort of Basque activist, isn't he?'

'I told you, Auguste said he isn't a Basque.'

'All right, what if he isn't? He's doing something for the Basques, they're paying him. That must be why José keeps checking up on him.'

I had told him about my latest meeting with José Zumárraga.

Maurice went on: 'Didn't he say he'd got hold of an Irish passport? Well, everyone knows there's an IRA-ETA connection. Perhaps he *is* Irish.'

'Oh come on. That can't be right. José hates the ETA. He told us that in Ondárroa.'

'Well, I don't know.'

'And Paco speaks English like an American . . . '

'And Spanish like a Mexican, and French like a Canadian. So. What does all that prove?'

'That he's a Puerto Rican with an Irish American mother, who has lived in Quebec.' I was joking. Oddly enough I now believe I had it just about right.

I tried once more: 'Maurice, I wish you'd tell me all you know.'

'What makes you think I haven't?'

'You knew we were going to run into him at Nájera. You knew just when. You were opening the door for him.'

156

'Quite the Sherlock Holmes, aren't we? I thought you'd worked it out that it was José at Ondárroa who told me to watch out there for Blas.'

'That was over a week before.'

'So?'

'But it was so exact – the time we arrived and everything.'

He sat for a moment drumming the bottom of his glass on the table in desperation, then he flung his head up: 'Archie, for Christ's sake, leave me alone. You'll only make things worse if you pry. If you're so curious, why don't you ask him when he comes?'

I left it at that. I think most people would have done: Maurice was very upset and I knew from experience that I'd get nowhere while he was; also I still felt oddly reassured by José's apparent approval that we were taking on Paco again. However foul Paco was, I felt whatever he was up to couldn't be too awful if José was part of it. I simply could not help liking the Basque from Ondárroa.

And when Paco did arrive – crunching through the gravel, tapping on the window at exactly half-past ten – he too worked to put my mind at rest.

I let him in; he swung his kit-bag on to the bunk and sat beside it as if he'd never been away, looked around him, at us both, then helped himself to a beer.

'Friends,' he began, then wiped his mouth on the back of his hand and belched, 'friends, I know you are taking me on this trip, this third trip I have had with you, with both of you fully conscious of what the nature of my ticket is, of how I've paid my fare. You can't like me for it one bit.' He gave me his twisted grin and then, God help me, put his hand firmly on my knee. 'But like it or not you're stuck with me for a day or two, and I think we ought to try to get on as well as we can. Now, to show you I'm sincere in this, truly sincere, here are three things I'll do for you. One: I'll tell you why I'm going to

157

Santiago. There's a conference of separatist leaders to be held there, and I aim to be at the table even though I'm not, as you once put it Archie, *persona grata* in this country; I aim to be there. Don't you worry how, I'll manage when I get there – that's my problem. But you'll get me there because no guardia or policeman is going to search an English van out of all the thousands of vehicles converging on Santiago by the end of the week. Two: here's the photo, and here's the letter Maurice wants.' He tapped his leather jacket. 'Right, Maurice? You'll have these as soon as you drop me where I want to be dropped. Three: this,' and he undid his kit-bag and pulled a bottle of Chivas Regal from the top. 'OK? Now if Archie will get out some fresh glasses, we'll see about getting friendly all over again.'

The rest of the journey to Santiago was not pleasant, at least not to begin with. From León, through Astorga and Ponferrada the reconstructed Camino coincides with one of the busiest roads in Spain, the N VI which carries the Galician fish and dairy products in an endless chain of lorries to Madrid and the western half of the centre of Spain. It is murder to drive on. After Astorga, mountains with steep hills and bends alternate with long rolling valleys filled with vines – neither landscape makes the flow of traffic any easier to deal with. We stopped at Astorga to buy the buttery sponge cakes – *mantecados* – which were worth it, and to look at Gaudi's Bishop's Palace, which was not. It's straight out of Disney Land. At Ponferrada a traffic policeman stopped me for going through a red light I had missed; I had been trying to read a rather ambiguous series of road signs.

Maurice talked us out of a spot fine; Paco remained glum and silent in the back. When at last we got away he said: 'Man, for a moment I thought you were pulling a fast one – trying to hand me over to the pigs before I could stop you. You wouldn't do that, now would you?'

158

The next day, Friday the twenty-third, was better to begin with. We were back on minor roads again and most of the through traffic was now going our way, all the way, pilgrims (for want of a better word) like us. Most interesting were the young people who had entered into the spirit of the thing and were actually walking or cycling. Many were dressed like Moni and Lili in black felt hats with cockle-shells – only forty, then thirty, then twenty miles to do to get there by midnight on the twenty-fourth.

Maurice and I discussed Moni and Lili, wondered how they were getting on.

Paco suddenly interrupted: 'That's fine, that's very nice what they're doing. But if we should happen to pass them and they want a lift, you just drive on. All right?'

'Whatever you say,' I replied, 'but there is room for them . . . '

'No hitch-hikers. The fewer people see me with you the better – that's obvious. And especially none of our friends from Pau who know me.'

I drove on feeling disturbed – partly because during this exchange I had felt Maurice tensing up again, worrying about something, and I still did not know what.

The countryside improved. The hills were steep, the views from the passes breath-taking, and everything green again, greener even than the Basque country, and far less parched than England or Normandy. We saw bullock carts with solid wheels bringing in wheat – men with bagpipes walked in front, whether to celebrate the harvest or scare off approaching traffic, I don't know. We stopped at the last town before Santiago, a place called Arzúa, for coffee and to stretch our legs, and suddenly I caught a sense of arrival: the windows were full of posters or stickers in Spanish and Galician welcoming *Los Reyes* – Juan Carlos and Sofía; their portraits were everywhere, many of them of the Queen on her own. What a clever image the most popular photograph of her is – combining the touching vulnerability and dignity of a madonna with the glossiness of the classier sort of film-star. Maurice quite cheered up at the sight of it, suggested we should be able to pick up a copy at the Santiago tourist office. There were also the official medals for Holy Year on sale – a silver cockle-shell with a red cross of Sant'Iago on it: again Maurice wanted one, but I insisted he should wait until we got there.

About three miles from Santiago the road, the Camino, crosses a ridge. From this ridge the pilgrim sees the city stretched below him for the first time, and so the ridge is called Mount Joy. As we approached its crest the flow of traffic slowed; lights – blue and orange – flashed ahead; a Guardia motioned us to slow down. A police siren wailed.

Just over the crest we saw the reason. A red Renault 4L had apparently driven off the road, over a shallow ditch, and into a tree. The front of the car was very badly smashed indeed.

'Christ,' cried Maurice. 'Oh, dear God.'

'Whatever is it?' I asked.

'That 4L. Didn't you see the number?'

'No?'

'It was French. Sixty-four – Pyrénées Atlantiques. It was Auguste and Jeanne-Marie, I'm sure of it.' He turned and looked at Paco, eyes suddenly wide with horror.

Paco was looking straight ahead, between us, down the road towards Santiago.

'Just drive on,' he ordered. 'There's nothing we can do.'

I did as he said.

PART FOUR

Santiago

CHAPTER 21

Paco directed us through a small complex of ring-roads and roundabouts, then a brief suburb of concrete or stuccoed appartments, and finally down a hill which left the rock on which the old town is built rising on our right. Flights of stone steps led down to our level and then, requiring a hair-pin turn to get on it, a cobbled road. Paco told me to take this and I managed it, but at the expense of a barrage of blasts from two buses – there seemed to be a small bus station at the foot of the hill.

'Park as soon as you can,' Paco said.

The steep road opened out into a small square – I pulled in behind a pick-up truck into which peasants were loading net sacks filled with tiny bright green peppers.

'Parking here seems to be restricted,' I said. The notice apparently forbade waiting during market hours without a permit.

'It doesn't matter. An English car, the big fiesta just about to start, nobody will bother you.'

'I hope you're right. A parking ticket on top of everything else is more than I want.'

'I've told you – it will be all right.'

Maurice and I turned in the front seats and faced him.

'Now what?' asked Maurice. 'We've brought you here, haven't we?'

'And you want your photo and so on, yes?' Paco grinned, tapped his jacket pocket. 'Well perhaps yes, perhaps no. Or rather, not quite yet. I want you to do just one or two more things for me, then you will get them. I want you to stay parked here for forty-eight hours exactly – until five o'clock on Sunday; and I want you to leave

163

me a spare set of keys, so I can come and go as I please until that time. Then, if you have not moved the van, at five o'clock on Sunday I will put the keys and your personal papers into an envelope and post them to you *poste restante* here at Santiago, and you will be able to pick them up at the *Correos* on Monday. You will not see me again after that, you'll be able to forget all about me, you'll be able to enjoy your holiday. How about that?'

'We haven't much choice, have we?' I grunted.

'We can come and go from here as we please?' asked Maurice.

'Of course. It's your van; I'm not stealing it from you or anything. I only want the keys so I can do the same – leave it locked, but come back when I like.'

'Come on then, Archie, let's get out.'

I was surprised at the sudden note of determination in his voice.

'Hang on – money, passports, guide. Be with you in a sec. You've got your keys, have you?'

'Yes.'

I handed mine over to Paco and joined Maurice on the pavement.

He took my arm and walked off briskly. 'I'm sorry, I just can't stand being with that awful man a moment longer than I have to, and when he said he wasn't handing over those things yet, I thought I was going to scratch his eyes out.'

'Where are we going?'

He stopped, looked at me, ran his long white fingers through his thick black hair. 'I'd like to try to find out if that crashed 4L was Jeanne-Marie's, see if we can help at all.'

'Of course.'

What followed was tedious. We found the headquarters of the municipal police quite easily, on the outskirts of the old town; with a little more difficulty got into the

164

traffic section. Patiently Maurice explained that we had seen a crashed car, that we thought might belong to friends. He described the car – French Renault 4L, red, sixty-four number plate. The pleasant, would-be-helpful, rather grey and elderly officer behind the desk took this all down, went away for more than ten minutes during which a queue of four or five more people formed behind us, came back at last with a smile on his face and said: 'You are very lucky, very lucky. No car of the sort you have described has been crashed in the precincts of the city for the last three months – I have checked all the records. So your friend is well.'

Maurice explained again that we had actually seen the car in question only an hour or so earlier, with its bonnet crumpled right up, its windscreen smashed, against a tree three miles outside the town. Perhaps the report had not yet been filed.

'Five kilometres?' the policeman repeated. 'You did not say that;' (though Maurice swore later that he had) 'then it is outside the city bounds. You need the Guardia Civil.'

At that point I wanted to give up – I fear and detest the Guardia Civil. But Maurice, albeit a little paler now, insisted that we follow it through.

We took a taxi. The Guardia outside the Cuartel was young, immaculate as they always are, clutched an automatic rifle with bayonet fixed between white-gloved hands, and was quite at a loss to know what to do about two importunate foreigners who wanted to get past him. However, he soon realised that it was the traffic branch that we wanted – unfortunately the Cuartel de Tráfico was three kilometres away, the other side of town. No, he did not know where we could get a taxi; no, certainly not, he would not leave his post to phone for one.

At that moment two senior officers came clattering down the stairs behind him – very self-important with brief-cases, shiny shoes, bald patches like tonsures just showing beneath their black patent leather hats, and fixed to their shiny leather belts neat little black holsters as harmless looking as purses.

'What is the problem?' they asked. Maurice told them and the result was a lift the whole way in a large dark green Seat that smelled of leather, expensive tobacco, and after-shave lotion. It was when we were sitting behind them in this luxury that we both noticed the bald patches.

'I hope no one we know sees us in here,' Maurice whispered, struggling to suppress the giggles, as we cruised, often saluted, through the narrow, crowded streets.

One of the officers put his arm on his seat back and looked over his shoulder at us and said, in not unreasonable English: 'It is very crowded you see and occupied. Tomorrow, the Kings will come in the evening and everything will be very occupied and especially the Forces of Law and Order also.'

'Your English is good,' I said.

'Oh no,' he smiled. 'I study for promotion.'

He had an orange mole on his left cheek.

At the Cuartel de Tráfico we began to get somewhere, perhaps because we had arrived in such state. They found for us one of the patrolmen who had attended the accident and was at that moment filing his report. Yes, the 4L was French, had a sixty-four number plate. As far as he knew there had been only one occupant, the driver, an elderly man apparently.

Why apparently?

Because he had been taken off to the hospital in an ambulance before the Guardia and his colleague arrived.

Wasn't this unusual?

Unusual yes – but by no means unheard-of. It was perfectly correct for the ambulance men to carry off any victims in need of medical attention before the arrival of the police if they were there first. It did not happen often but – he shrugged – in this case it had. One of the

166

ambulance men had stayed behind and had told him that the injured person was about sixty years old, grey-haired, dressed in black, looked like a priest. Many priests came from France for El Día de Santiago.

Maurice remained persistent. Later he told me he had a 'feel' about the crashed car; Jeanne-Marie's 4L had often been parked outside the flat in Pau, and so was very familiar to him – he had occasionally ridden in it; although there must be hundreds of red 4Ls registered in Pyrénées Atlantiques, he had felt sure the crashed one was the same.

Had the officer seen any documents?

Here, I feel sure, if we had not arrived with two high-ranking officers, we should have been told firmly, though no doubt politely, to leave. However, a little grudgingly, the patrolman produced a plastic wallet, the sort garages give you to file servicing invoices in.

'This is all,' he said. 'No doubt the rest – identity card, insurance and so on were in the injured man's pocket or luggage and are up at the hospital.'

The plastic wallet had been issued by *Jean Broqué S.A., Votre Concessionaire Renault, Route de Tarbes à Pau* and stated clearly that the owner of the vehicle was Mlle Jeanne-M Castets.

A short walk took us to the hospital and final frustration. The receptionist at the enquiry desk was a woman, very kind, very precise, very firm. She listened attentively to everything Maurice said and then swung her chair round to face her switchboard and made two quick calls, then swung back to us. I know her well now, of course; she smiles like a friend every time I pass her on my twice daily visits.

There had been one person only in the French 4L: a Monsieur Paul Vayron, a curé from Bizanos, near Pau. He had just received extensive surgery and was now in the intensive care unit. It was assuredly absolutely out of the question to see him. No, it would be most improper for us to see any documents he had been carrying. The hospital had no reason to doubt their patient's identity – after all his card had a photograph, and although there were severe facial injuries there were no inconsistencies. Any further inquiries must go through the proper channels. If Señor Vayron *was* a friend of ours the hospital would keep us up-to-date on his condition and allow us to see him as soon as he was able to receive visitors; if, as it seemed, the reverend gentleman was not known to us, then she could not see what further business of ours his condition was – surely we should simply be grateful that no friend of ours had been hurt, and leave it at that.

By then I was ready to agree with her. Reluctantly Maurice followed me out. He stood on the pavement, brow deeply furrowed, then shrugged and agreed – yes, a beer would be a good idea.

We worried over the whole business in the nearest bar for the length of one beer and then agreed to shelve it, though Maurice remained convinced that Auguste at least, and possibly Jeanne-Marie too had been in the 4L and had somehow been spirited away. Why? He shrugged, and muttered something about Paco Blas not being a Basque. I wouldn't swallow it: that two people should have disappeared as a result of collusion between ambulance men, Guardia Civil, and an unspecified number of hospital staff, just did not seem possible. It was self-evident as far as I was concerned that whoever the 4L belonged to, Auguste and Jeanne-Marie had not been in it when it crashed.

We wandered slowly back into the town, and, although to begin with we were still a little sulky with each other, and at the back of our minds the presence of Paco in the van continued to nag, we soon cheered up.

The centre of Santiago is of course the Cathedral and the surrounding complex of squares, monasteries and palaces as splendid an area as you'll find anywhere in Europe, though we did not penetrate properly to it until the following morning. Three streets linked by alleys, roughly parallel to each other but converging towards the Cathedral, run through the old town and we found ourselves wandering about these, and as we did our spirits rose.

Closed to traffic, two of them with arcades, they were filling with a slow-moving but quietly excited throng of pilgrims – and a more mixed crowd I don't think I have ever seen: every race I am sure was represented, every age group, every class. Americans in floppy hats strummed guitars (did we see the man, woman, and little girl from Pamplona? I think so – certainly I ran into them the following day), a flock of Japanese nuns floated by, beef-red Australians festooned with cameras, some Austrians in *lederhosen* and woollen stockings – had they walked the whole way? Very possibly – and large Spanish families tricked out in their spick and span best with swarms of children. A bishop in magenta silks rustled across our path with obsequious chaplains in tow: a pair of municipal policemen saluted him smartly, and a couple from Bradford, the man tall like a heron, tried to snap him but he was gone too quickly, his red skull cap bobbing above the crowd.

The narrowest, most serpentine of the three streets is the street of bars and restaurants: Calle del Franco – of the Frenchman, nothing to do with the Dictator. Here the windows are filled with elaborate displays of sea-food – spider crabs, prawns, langoustines, mussels, clams, less easily identified objects of dark green and purple, and always at the centre either Sant'Iago's cockle-shells or a huge octopus, coral pink and cream, crimson towards the body, arranged with its tentacles flowing like streams of bubbling lava from a cratered centre.

The scallops are absurdly expensive – who does not want to eat Coquilles St Jacques on St James's Day? – the

169

octopus cheap. In one bar we had lumps of octopus cooked in small coarse earthenware dishes with a hot spicy sauce and in another a plate each of fresh mussels just scented with thyme and lemon; and everywhere Ribeira – the thin delicate white wine, slightly fizzy, not quite clear, served in shallow open china bowls called *cuncas*: delicious from the barrel but nearly always disappointing bottled.

We did not want to go back to the van, but we drifted away from the bars back into the arcaded Rúa del Villar where the King and Queen looked down at us from every shop window – usually serious, conscious of the cares of state; the Queen occasionally with her Madonna smile as if done by Filippo Lippi. Galicia welcomes the Kings, said stickers everywhere, in Galician as well as Spanish, and Maurice remembered he wanted the poster of the Queen, asked if we could go to the Tourist Office.

On the way, a sudden flurry in the crowd – two youths pushed past us, ran up to a large wooden door and swiftly, with hammer and nails, fastened a painted cloth to it, threw a handful of bills on the floor, and were gone.

The home-made banner announced that the *Movemento Comunista de Galicia* called for a *Goberno Provisional Galego* and the duplicated bills said 'Let the Twenty-fifth be the Day of Galicia, not the Day of Spain'.

Outside the Tourist Office we found ourselves looking at a poster advertising *Festivales de España 1976, Santiago de Compostela, Iglesia de San Francisco, 21 al 29 de Julio, 22.30 horas*, a different show each night, ballet, concerts, theatre and for tonight Friday the 23rd, the *Compañía Nacional de Teatro* in *Julio César, obra de W. Shakespeare*.

'Let's go,' said Maurice.

'It doesn't *start* till ten-thirty.'

'So? This is Spain – and ten-thirty is the *right* time to start an evening's fun.'

'I shall fall asleep in the middle, or even earlier.'

'Archie, don't be such a stick-in-the-mud.' He struck an attitude: 'Would you were fatter: you read much, you're a great observer, and you look quite through the deeds of men – and you love *no* plays. Oh come on Archie, let's go to the play.'

'Wherever did you get all that from?'

'I played the part of Caesar at school once, did I not tell you?'

'It was a brute part of Brutus to kill so capital a calf as thee.'

'Boom-boom. Shall we go in?'

But inevitably all the seats were sold; however, Maurice did get his poster of Queen Sofía. Poor boy, it looks like the nearest he'll get to actually seeing her.

CHAPTER 22

First light in the morning woke me. It was possible to curtain off the back part of the van completely, but I was again on the front seats, as I had been at night since Paco had rejoined us. I lay where I was for a time hoping I would go back to sleep, but I was very uncomfortable, conscious too that I was clearly visible to anyone who looked in; I was none too warm either.

I hoisted myself up, peeped through the curtain behind me. In the gloom I could make out Maurice's head, his black hair spread on the pillow – high time he had a trim, I thought. I could hear the steady breathing of Paco from the bunk. There was a sour smell of stale sweat and unwashed clothes: another reason for fervent hopes that Paco would really do as he promised this time and leave us within the next thirty-six hours.

Under my blanket I pulled on what clothes I had taken off, and let myself out, shutting the door as quietly as I could. I set off down the dewy deserted streets towards the Cathedral. One, then two, then perhaps four or five clocks at varying distances began to strike. Seven o'clock, a dawn only apparently late because of the adjusted hour.

The sky was shifting from bluey-grey to lilac, a few bars of white cloud hung high overhead but still untouched by direct light; then, as I looked, even further above them, a vapour trail spread like a slow crack: it caught the sun, glowed gold fire as if a furnace existed beyond the porcelain of the sky and the fault had given a glimpse of it. I shook my head vigorously. I am not normally prone to apocalyptic fancies.

I took a slow walk round the Cathedral, starting from

the south and walking to the east, leaving the west front till last. It's a big building, a complex of buildings, with hospices, palaces, monasteries and so on tacked on to it, and it's on different levels so to get round one goes up and down several wide flights of stone steps, in and out at least four squares.

The first of these has a small fountain with sea-horses in the centre and rows of silversmiths round the outside; the shop windows are filled with treasure – most of it conventional enough in design, but beautifully finished and displayed – St James again and again, as Pilgrim and as *Matamoros* – the killer of Moors – on a white horse, scallop shells, silver models of Santiago's monuments, and other things more generally Spanish – hunting-dogs pointing, fighting bulls, Quixotes and Sanchos, and of course holy medals by the hundred; and in amongst all this silver there were nodes of gleaming jet carved into rosary beads or tiny statuettes. It's a little easy for an Anglo-Saxon protestant to be superior to all this: but perhaps there's more sense and sensibility in having on your sideboard a well-turned image of Sant'Iago or a fighting bull than a dish-washer in your kitchen; and anyway the sheer profusion was a delight.

I had woken up with a knot of sour anxiety at the root of my throat – it was beginning to dissolve now as I turned away from the silversmiths' windows. The morning was already a little warmer, a few people were now moving about – mostly heading up the flight of steps ahead of me – but not enough of them to stir the strutting pigeons into flight. I followed them up and found I was facing a tall granite doorway surrounded by the brusque, faintly comic images of the tenth century. It was open. The people I had seen were hurrying through it into a world of gold and crimson, of incense and bright chandeliers, of silver and gilt plate and heavy brocades, of the Mass said for the Vigil of St James.

I hesitated, decided I would rather explore the inside

173

with Maurice, and climbed up more steps into the top half of the next square. Here I paused, at the east end of the Cathedral, and looked around. Below me what should have been a splendid vista back to the Square of Silversmiths with its fountain was spoiled somewhat by rows of collapsible wooden chairs and scaffolding – a sort of open air theatre.

To my left was the blank prison-like wall of a convent, but to my right were what looked like cloisters fenced off by a magnificent screen of bronze and granite, sur-mounted – *naturally* – by Sant'Iago as pilgrim; and beyond, seen now from behind, but no less impressive for that, towering above the roofs and domes of the whole Cathedral that lay between me and them, the huge twin towers of the west end, topped with columns, obelisks, and more domes, and hung with giant bells.

Down steps this time into the next square. In front of me a huge monastery or hospice with a statue of St Martin of Tours slicing up his cloak high up on the façade. I remembered: the main branch of the mediaeval Camino started at Tours, and for millions of French, Scandinavians, and Britons ended here, in this huge inn. Behind me was the north face of the Cathedral, the least Spanish, a slice of rococo Rome.

It's all too much, I thought, and of course I'd left the best to last. A turn or two down narrow streets between tall blank walls brought me out between two palaces and thus into the Plaza del Obradoiro.

It is huge. Facing me was the long façade of the classical Town Hall, surmounted by a giant limestone statue in the style of Bernini, of Sant'Iago handing it out with sword and the hooves of his horse to sundry distressed Moors; across the far end was the less grandiose but still splendid College of St Jerome. I walked into the middle of the Square towards the centre, and then turned – first to the north, to the tricksy splendour of the plateresque frontage of what is now apparently one of the best hotels in Europe, the Hotel de los Reyes Católicos; and then to the east.

And here I must confess to a brief moment of irritation.

Zig-zagging, interlocking flights of stairs and balustrades lead the eye to the great west door. Square towers, beautifully proportioned, frame it; heaped splendours of angels, saints, columns, pilasters, cornices, arches, and every conceivable device in the rhetoric of baroque architecture are its back drop; and set just behind it rise up the giant spires – each one comprising three columned, fluted towers set one on top of the other, the last one hung with bells and topped off with a fantasy of balustrades and obelisks with, on the very top, and hung, as it were, on a needle point of stone, a gilt ball and cross.

What irritated was the fact that the great west door that all this was meant to set off was now masked by a wooden structure, painted in red and white horizontal stripes, comprising a sort of pantomime façade representing, as far as I could tell from the rows of arches and the cut-out domes topped off with crescents, a Moorish mosque – possibly the one at Córdoba. It took me a moment to recall what it was all about; then it came back to me. What I was looking at was the *fachada*, the main piece of the *Fuego del Apóstol*, the *pièce de résistance* of the gigantic firework display that would take place in the evening – the opening of the Festival of St James in Holy Year.

Irritation evaporated in interest; I walked nearer, quizzically. Workmen were already out adding the finishing touches – yes, one could see on the sill of each arch a white cylinder the size of a large paint tin – no doubt some of the actual fireworks. It was a relief really: I had vaguely thought that this traditional illumination would be mounted on the actual fabric of the Cathedral – I saw now that this temporary confection from the Arabian Nights was a much better idea.

175

I turned and looked back over the Square. How many would it hold? Thirty thousand? The King and Queen would watch, of course. Probably from the long balcony on the Town Hall – a better view than the one from the hotel where, no doubt, they would be staying. We must be here early, I thought, to find a spot from which we can see both the Kings and the fireworks. I smiled to myself, as one does when one has a surprise gift to offer – Maurice is going to love a touch of royalty in the night.

Already gone eight. Time to get back. Leaving the Plaza I passed two long high green lorries, parked up under the south end of the façade, RTVE emblazoned on their sides – Radio Televisión de España – of course they would be here, no doubt covering the whole tour, but certainly the royal arrival and the ceremony tomorrow in the Cathedral. The King, as I understood it, was to give a special message to the nation from the Apostle's Tomb itself.

Leaving the Plaza I took one last look back across to the Town Hall and the hotel. There was more life now – a couple of limousines had entered the Square, some blinds had gone up, shutters opened. Four men in uniform, peaked caps, moved from the car to the centre and looked around them. They carried a radio transmitter; a long antenna whipped in the air above them. One of them pointed, I followed his finger, and briefly something moved up on the Town Hall roof, near the giant statue. Security. Something of a problem, I said to myself, taking into consideration all the factors – darkness, thirty thousand spectators, an exposed balcony, and fireworks.

CHAPTER 23

It is my firm belief that human beings outside history books, memoirs, biographies, and the lesser fiction, are absurdly fallible, always ready to be fooled in the most blatant and obvious ways, capable of seeing only the familiar, prone to ignore the unusual, desiring always to see what they want and ignoring for as long as they can the difficult, the puzzling, the problematic, the dangerous. Hence the success of conjurors, *Coronation Street*, confidence tricksters, and democratically elected politicians. Hence also the failure of a bureaucratic, centralised, dehumanised, greedy society to pay any attention at all to the few cranks who care about our slow, irreversible collapse into environmental disaster.

If this is so, then I am truly not more than averagely stupid not to have realised then, as I walked back to the van, that Paco Blas was in Santiago to kill the King. Not even more than averagely stupid not to have realised it a little later when Maurice told me that our guest had spent most of the time since I had gone cleaning and servicing his American automatic rifle.

Since few people can be unaware of the fact that Juan Carlos I and Sofía his wife survived the night of the twenty-fourth of July 1976, not only survived it, but survived it as far as I know without even realising an attempt had been made on their lives, I don't suppose anyone who has read as far as this will bother now to go on. Still, I shall finish it. There is just a chance that Maurice will live, and be able to read again, and I think he'll enjoy it. It seems he really might recover from the two shattered legs, the internal injuries, and the state of almost unbroken coma he has been in for nearly a week now. The doctor was more cheerful about him today, and it did seem to me that his eyes, open for one of their brief spells, focused on me and that his fingertips responded to the pressure of mine.

When I got back to the van, Maurice was making coffee – or standing at the stove watching the *cafetera* doing it for him. As I entered through the back door which was now unlocked, he looked up at me – pale again, his eyelids bruised looking – then he flinched away, back to the pot, which was beginning to bubble.

'That smells good,' I said.

'Oh! I thought you'd have had something in a caff.'

'Well, I haven't, so I hope there's some for me.' I looked at the bunk. The thin blanket that usually covered it was spread neatly over it, though there were odd lumps, contours, beneath it. Not, however, those of a person. 'Paco's gone then?'

'He went out. He said he'd be gone for an hour or so.'

Maurice lifted down a second cup from its hook above the gas-ring, put it beside the one already there.

'Did you have a nice walk?'

'Yes, fine. I went right round the outside of the Cathedral.'

'Then you won't want to do it again.'

'Yes. Yes, of course I will.'

He poured coffee.

'Don't ask me how I've been,' he said.

'How have you been?'

'Fine. Just fine.' He turned and faced me at last. 'It's been fascinating watching Paco clean out his gun, and all that. As if he meant to use it today,' and, somewhat dramatically, he flicked the coverlet off the bunk.

The gun was there – the M14, 7.62mm fully automatic rifle I had examined before. There were three magazines, one clipped into the gun, another lying near it, the third much further away, up near the pillow.

The lump of anxiety I had woken up with resolidified with harder, sharper edges than ever.

'Not long after you'd gone – I suppose you thought I was asleep – *he* got up too. And he dug that lot out of his kit-bag and went over it all very carefully. For a time I thought I should pretend to be asleep. I mean, I didn't want to embarrass him – ' This was said with horribly bitter sarcasm ' – but he caught me peeping, and when he did he bloody winked at me.'

I didn't know what to say. Maurice gulped and went on.

'Then he went out. Said he had to get some things. Said he'd be an hour. Do you know what I did then?'

'No.'

'I had a look at it. At all that lot. I was careful how. I don't think he'll notice.'

'Why did you do that?'

'Curious. Horrible fascination. All that sort of thing. Do you know what I discovered?'

'No.'

'Two of those box things – magazines? – are full with bullets with the ends on. Live? Is that the right word? The third is less than full and the bullets have no ends on. Blanks. That's it, isn't it?'

I picked up the two loose magazines. Both were full, with live ammunition.

'Then he's put the one with blanks in in the gun,' I said.

'No,' said Maurice. 'I did. I changed them round. Do you think he'll notice?'

'Why did you do that?'

'Someone might get hurt, else.'

I drank some coffee.

'I don't see why he's got a magazine half full with blanks,' I said at last.

Maurice looked at me over his cup.

'Don't you?' he said. 'They're left over from the gun-battle at Nájera. Hadn't you guessed? That wasn't real you know. Just pretend.'

I felt too confused to sort out the right comment or question to that straightaway, and before I could think of anything Paco came bustling back in again. It wasn't until much later in the day that I worked out the significance of what Maurice had said.

Paco was carrying two parcels and an envelope. One of the parcels was large, loose, and softish. The other rectangular, hard, not so big. The envelope was just an envelope. It was addressed to: 'Señor Francisco Blas, Lista Correos, Santiago de Compostela.' I could read this because he dropped it on the table in front of me.

'My, you two are looking grumpy. Anything wrong?'

We said nothing.

'*Joder*, I get it. You've been peeking – ' (Sing-song voice, for naughty infants) ' – You've been looking at my toys. Now Archie. Maurice. Don't you worry about them. You knew I had a gun. You've seen it before. And I just felt it needed a clean-out. But today, as far as you're concerned, I'm no gunman at all. I'm just a plain ordinary ETA Basque Separatist attending the conference here. Right? Just you quote me if ever you're asked.'

I've just noted that one believes what one wants to believe, and I believed him. I don't think Maurice did. But then Maurice already knew a lot more about him than I.

We finished our coffee and Paco opened the mail he had brought from the post office. The large squashy parcel contained a one-piece green denim overall; the rectangular one a cardboard box – he checked what was in it without taking it from the tissue in which it was wrapped, so I didn't see what it was. He put the box down near the gun. The envelope contained a card mounted in transparent plastic – again I couldn't see it clearly, but it had a small photo in the corner, was some sort of identity card or pass. Perhaps, I thought, a pass to the conference. He slipped it into the top pocket of the overall.

180

'Great,' he said, when he had finished. 'That's all very fine, very well put together.'

Then he set about dismantling the rifle again and as he did he continued to talk feverishly, cracking silly jokes, sweating slightly. He was obviously excited, and almost high with it, which may be why he did not appear to notice Maurice's switch of the magazines – not that anything was likely to be achieved by it: the magazines, like all the other parts, were slotted into special compartments stitched into the kit-bag.

He ended by pulling a lanyard tight and then a zipper which he locked into place. 'There, you see,' straightening as he snapped the lock, 'it's all gone to bye-byes.'

'I must say I'm relieved,' I said.

'Yes? Well, I suppose they are frightening things to have around if you're not used to them. Now, friends, I must go out again for an hour or so. Er . . . you will lock up if you go too, won't you? Great. Be seeing you around, I guess,' and off he went, leaving overall and kit-bag on the bunk.

Maurice had sat white-lipped and silent through all this. Now he shifted his head to check Paco had really gone out of ear-shot – I too could see the close-cropped curly black head disappearing behind a huge sack of potatoes a porter was humping into the market – then he looked back at me.

'It was rather silly of him to say what he did earlier.'

'Say what?'

'That he's "a plain ordinary ETA Basque Separatist".'

'Because we might give him away?'

'No, silly knickers. Because once you're that close to the ETA, you know there's no such thing.'

'I don't follow.'

'Look,' he rummaged in the file where he kept his *realia* and brought out a magazine – *Cuadernos* – found the page he wanted. 'I got this for old Stukely, thought he'd be interested. It says the ETA movement is divided against itself into about six different factions. There's the ETA Zarra, the ETA Berri. There's the ETA V, and ETA VI, and there's the LCR-ETA VI who put out that pamphlet I picked up in Pamplona. Here. Remember?'

The evening he disappeared and got stoned – I remembered.

'I don't see why Paco should go into all that for us,' I said. 'I mean he'd hardly expect us to understand, let alone be interested.'

'No? Perhaps you're right. It's just that it's really impossible to say "plain ordinary ETA" if you're on the inside. And if he really is going to this conference as any sort of ETA rep he'd be going as rep of one of these factions – they'd never agree to one representative for all of them.'

'If he's not going to this conference as an ETA rep, what is he up to?'

He shrugged: 'I don't know. At least, I don't think I do. At any rate it's not really our business, is it? I mean, none of it's anything to do with us?'

'Of course not.'

Nevertheless he went back to chewing on his nails.

I thought over what he had said for thirty seconds, and decided we were both suffering from self-inflicted paranoia: it seemed time to get out and enjoy ourselves.

CHAPTER 24

Churches in Spain are like the bars – either dark or bright. The difference is that the dark bars are better than the bright ones, while with churches it is the other way about. The cathedral of Santiago de Compostela is a bright church, perhaps the brightest of all.

For a start the baroque façades are just that: inside it is twelfth-century romanesque or earlier – clean, light, for a Spanish church relatively uncluttered. During the festivities it is bright with gleaming silver and gilt, crimson carpets, white altar cloths. Chandeliers coruscate as you walk beneath them, candles flutter in the stir set up by gold vestments. If you're lucky you will find they are swinging the enormous silver censer, six and a half feet high, suspended from the dome a hundred and thirty feet above – an impressive object even when it's not in use.

Sant' Iago himself watches all this from a gilded throne set in a marble niche above and beyond the high altar. He is simply carved, polychrome, clad in a silver mantle encrusted with precious stones, and you're encouraged to walk up into his little chamber to kiss this cloak. Whether you do or not is up to you, but from here you can peep out over his shoulder down the long wide nave, punctuated with chandeliers, back to the west door.

The place has a unity – much of it is the work of one man, a master architect and sculptor known as Mateo, who, for my money, did a better job on Santiago than Michelangelo and Bernini did on St Peter's. His masterpiece is the Pórtico de la Gloria at the west end.

This is a vaulted porch, a twelfth-century doorway, enclosed now by the baroque screen I had seen from the outside on my morning walk. The screen is not only a shell protecting the Pórtico from the weather – it also carries a surprising area of clear glass which lights Mateo's work with daylight, and from late morning onwards the slow swing of sunlight plays across the central figures, subtly picking out each one in turn.

In current art jargon, the Pórtico is an 'environment' – to see it one has to be in it. Inside, facing the nave, Christ Transfigured, surrounded by angels, fills the tympanum above a figure of St James. Here all is solemn, dignified, touched with awe. Behind, on the pillars supporting the west side of the vault, mortal figures stand – kings, queens, bishops – facing, like you, the Holy Mysteries in front of them. Then, as the eye moves up over the arches and down the pillars flanking the Christ the figures become more and more openly rich and varied, expressions of humanity as vigorous as you will find in the *Canterbury Tales.*

There's more to it than this, and I hope to go back to it with Maurice one day. This may happen. It seems he had a good night last night and he quite definitely does recognise me now through all the tubes up his nose and in his arm and so on. I think he will get better.

There is one particular figure, though, that stays in my mind, even after that single visit. Behind the central column which supports St James and the Christ in Glory, behind it and therefore actually in the Cathedral, is a kneeling figure which faces the high altar, far away at the end of the nave. It is only when one realises that this figure is a self-portrait of Mateo himself, that one begins to sense the inexhaustible significance of the Pórtico: Mateo, in stone, offers his visible, hand-hewn world to the Invisible Glory of his carving strives to represent.

Two small queues form around the Pórtico. One leads up to the figure of St James. In amongst the stone fruits, plants, beneath his feet, five smooth holes have been worn through seven centuries, for here each pilgrim puts his hand and says within himself whatever he feels the need to say at the end of the Camino. Good Christians believe the Virgin herself has made this pilgrimage and put her hand there, and I must believe the Wife of Bath did too. Only a churl would stand back in the face of two such precedents.

Not everyone, however, joins the other line – mainly it consists of mothers with children, but there are always a few older people, most of whom are just a little self-conscious, embarrassed, about what they're up to. Which is this: Mateo's head is on the level of a seven year old's head, say the level of my diaphragm. It is thought that if you touch your forehead to his, some of his inspiration will stick to you for a year at least and maybe for a life-time.

As Maurice said, one simply cannot afford not to give it a try: perhaps it's a way of showing gratitude.

None of our enjoyment was marred by the general bustle that was going on – pilgrims streaming in, hammers going on the *fachada* for the fireworks outside, workmen unrolling heavy cable, setting up lights and scaffolding for the next day's television broadcast – workmen, I might as well say it now though I did not then make the connection, dressed in green overalls.

I rather like cathedrals to be busy, even noisy, but I must say I was just a little shocked to hear our names called high and clear from half-way up the nave, but then really pleased to see the black felt hats, the piled rucksacks of Moni and Lili bobbing through the crowd towards us. Apart from anything else it meant we could take another turn round the Pórtico: Maurice explained it to them, they too had to carry out the rituals, it all seemed more and more like fun, and finally quite appropriate when Moni said: '*E-e-e-e-h bien*,' (with a full heavy Béarnais emphasis on the '-*en*') 'we made it. Now we celebrate.'

'*Avec champagne*,' said Lili, '*bien entendu*.'

On the way to the bar Moni asked me: 'Is Paco still with you?'

185

'Till tomorrow only.'

'All right. We don't have to meet him.'

The champagne – Spanish, drinkable and not too dear – was just right, the sea-food we ordered with it as appetisers perfect, the bar we were in jolly. For an hour or so we chatted and giggled, ordered another, became just a little high. Out of all the talk, then and at lunch, two passages were important.

Half-way through the second bottle Maurice brought up his fears about Auguste and Jeanne-Marie, was about to recount the story of our attempts to track them down, when Moni forestalled him by pulling a letter from the pocket in the seat of her jeans.

'Read this,' she declared, 'it was at the *Lista Correos*, the *poste restante*, for me this morning.'

It was from Jeanne-Marie. It described how Auguste had been approached in a café in Pau by an acquaintance from his days as a burglar who told him that Santiago would be a very dangerous place for him to be that month. Auguste had taken this to mean that someone would be in Santiago whom he might recognise, who did not want to be recognised. Such things could be serious, he had decided. So, they had sold the 4L to a darling old curé, had put together all their money, and were flying to Les Antilles for a fortnight instead.

'An' 'ow now we get to Lisbon?' said Lili, and pulled her French face.

We told them that Jeanne-Marie's 4L was crashed, that the curé was in the Intensive Care Unit at the hospital. It now seemed possible that this poor priest had been severely injured in error for Auguste. Why? By whom? It seemed Paco must be connected, but what could we do? For five minutes or so the champagne and the world turned sour.

A little later we moved on to a small restaurant where we ate well off Galician *empanadas* – pasties stuffed with

186

shell-fish – pork chops, and drank another couple of bottles. Then, just after I had ordered coffee, coñac, and anís, Moni noticed a small poster hanging on the wall near our table. It was the same as the one we had seen outside the Tourist Office the night before.

'That is a strange choice, is it not?' she said, and hiccupped politely behind her hand. '*Julio César*.'

'Why so strange?' I asked.

'*Julius Caesar* is a tragedy – I have studied it – because he is assass . . . assinass . . . murdered. That's right, isn't it?'

'Of course.'

'And Julius Caesar is J C is Juan Carlos.'

Maurice put down his glass and his finger-nails went to his mouth, but I paid no attention.

'Is it a threat or a warning?' Moni went on. 'A threat because he is a tyrant? Or a warning to would-be assinass . . . murderers?'

'*Qu'est-ce qui se passe?*' asked Lili. Moni explained.

Lili sat silent for a moment, head sparrow-like on one side, slowly chewing. Then she said in French: 'If he is murdered, it will not be because he is a tyrant, but because he is not enough of one.'

I reflected aloud that some players, not Shakespeare's lot, had got into trouble reviving *Richard II* to coincide with the Earl of Essex's ill-fated attempt at a coup, but none of them really followed what I was saying.

The coffee, coñac and anís arrived.

'Archie?' Maurice, rather pale, stood up. 'I don't want any more. I think . . . I think I'll go back to the van, and have . . . a lie-down. Do you mind?'

'Not at all, dear boy. I'll be with you soon.'

I had taken it into my head to explain to Lili, in French, that one could mix anís and coñac together, it makes a good drink, the Spanish call it *sol y sombra* . . . I embarked on this impossible enterprise, and Maurice went.

CHAPTER 25

I reached the van about forty minutes after Maurice had left the café. Moni and Lili had declined to come with me; their dislike of Paco prevented them. They told me they were staying in the Village of Nations just outside the town and we made a loose arrangements to meet up again at lunch-time the following day, same bar, same time. They insisted on paying half the not inconsiderable bill.

At the van there was, at first, no sign of Maurice, and I had no keys. I searched for a note and found these words, scrawled with a finger in the dust on the rear door: 'Our guest reads no plays, M'.

I stared at this for a long time, long enough for a traffic policeman to stare at me. It was no use – I needed a toilet, a drink of water, more coffee. I found all three in the nearest bar.

'Reads no plays' – the end of the 'Let me have men about me that are fat' speech from *Julius Caesar*, the speech describing Caesar's fear of Cassius, the assassin. Was Maurice telling me that Paco was an assassin, was about to kill someone? It seemed possible. It would explain why he had left his message phrased so obscurely – clearly he couldn't leave it in a way that Paco would understand if he came back before I did. Where was Maurice now? Presumably he had set about trying to do something to stop Paco. What? Go to the police? No. His message would have been different if he had, somehow he would have indicated that that was where he was; indeed he could have come back to the restaurant on his way and told me. No – for some reason I could not then fathom, the idiot boy had gone off on his own, and probably in a hurry since he had not returned to the restaurant to consult me.

If I was to help Maurice, who, if my reasoning was right, might well now be in considerable danger, I had to work out on my own who it was Paco Blas was trying to kill.

So far I think my brain had worked quite intelligently: but faced with this problem, far too much to drink and far too much to eat messed my reasoning. I should have realised that nine times out of ten Maurice would not be all that bothered about Paco's target. He had already said as much: 'None of it's anything to do with us, is it?' He had done as much as he could, in a general way, by swapping, ineffectually I felt sure, the magazine of blanks for the one of live ammunition. And I should have followed the Cassius hint the whole way.

I did neither of these things. A tired brain falls back on patterns. Earlier I had allowed myself to believe Paco's own statement about himself – that he was in Santiago to attend the conference of separatists, that he was a representative of the ETA. Who in Santiago, I asked myself, would the ETA wish to kill? Ransacking my memory, the answer I came up with was Rafael Llodio, the moderate, non-Marxist separatist who was gaining support at the expense of the ETA; Rafael Llodio who was at the conference Paco had said he was here to attend. My task now, it seemed to me, was to find out where the conference was being held.

I should add that I did not feel at all confident about this line of reasoning; I was in a state of despairing panic, felt I had to do something, and this was the best I could think of.

I thought of the police. But I felt sure things were urgent, that Maurice might be in immediate danger; I knew it would take me hours at least to get the police to understand what I was getting at. I couldn't have done it in French, let alone Spanish. No. If I was to be any use to the poor boy I would have to act on my own.

189

Out on the pavement again, I set my mind to working out the best way with my inability at spoken Spanish of finding out where the venue of the conference was, and was rudely interrupted by the waiter – I had not paid for my coffee. Then I remembered the newspaper where Maurice and I had first read of it – *El País*. It was just possible that today's edition would carry a further report; not possible, *likely* I told myself, since they had felt it worth mentioning a week before it was due to open. That came to me while I waited for my change.

It took me another ten minutes to find a newsagent selling the thing, another ten to fight my way through it, but I found what I was looking for. With the bastard sort of classical education I picked up in my youth, I can *read* most romance languages so long as what's written is reasonably simple. This was simple enough. The conference would open officially on Monday, 26th. Most representatives, including Rafael Llodio, were already in Santiago, and were already in informal session discussing procedure and an agenda. It was all happening at the Universidad de Santiago de Compostela, Facultad de Artes.

I actually knew where the University was, or at any rate what I took to be its principal building – barely two hundred yards from where the van was parked. In two minutes more I was breathlessly walking round the outside, trying to find the way in; the main front entrance – magnificent bronze doors in a renaissance façade – was firmly shut; however, round the side I found another, lesser gate that was open for tourists, and I had to pay fifty pesetas to get in.

I found myself in a splendid quadrangle with wide arcades; discreet notices directed me to *Los departamentos de Derecho*, *de Ciencas Sociales*, *de Lenguas Modernas*. Well, I was still rather drunk – and all that did not add up in my mind in the way it should have done. Instead, desperate, I approached a uniformed custodian, guide, or whatever and – '*¿Facultad de Artes?*' I tried.

'*Sí señor*,' the honest fellow replied.

'*No. ¿Donde está la Facultad de Artes?*'

'*Aquí, señor, aquí.*' He beamed cheerfully, and gestured broadly. Slowly the truth dawned on me.

'Ah,' I said. '*Toda esta localidad es la Facultad de Artes.*'

Not unnaturally this was lost on him, but he came back strongly and with an even bigger smile. 'You Eeeenglish? *Bueno.* Thees ees the Fagultee of Artes.' Again the broad gesture.

The ticket I had bought at the entrance said as much. '*Gracias, señor.*'

'*De nada, buenos días,*' a polite nod and he moved off.

Humiliation added bitterness to my desperation. It was quite beyond me to attempt the Spanish for 'Whereabouts in this large place is the probably illegal conference of separatists being held?' and better linguist than I though he was, I doubted if his English went that far.

And then, before I had time to consider my next move, I saw, coming towards me but still at the end of the long arcade, not Paco and Maurice, but unmistakable with his black beret, his short square figure, his rubber-shod stick – José Zumárraga.

My mind though drunk worked quickly; because drunk, stupidly. The connection I had made in my mind between José and Paco remained unbroken. I assumed that here, limping towards me, was Paco's accomplice and, though José had already recognised me, was smiling, calling, waving, I turned and began to run from him.

There was no clear way out down the side I was on. As I came to the corner I realised that José was heading across the cobbles in the centre, towards the fountain, to cut me off; moreover, a man who was with him broke into a trot behind me and was gaining. I moved off down the second side, saw I would not beat José to the far end, pushed on a large wooden door I was passing, and found that it was not fastened. I stumbled through.

I was in a large, well-appointed lecture hall. At the far

end, to the side of the lectern but on the rostrum was another door. I raced up to it, pulled, pushed, twisted at the handle – this one *was* locked. I sank down to the floor behind the lectern, curled up as small as I could, and waited; waited for the actual or would-be assassins of Rafael Llodio to find and kill me too. They were not long coming.

'*Entró por aquí.*'

'*Ya lo sé,*' José's voice, '*le vi entrar. ¿Hubiera salido por aquella puerta?*'

'*No lo sé. Vamos a ver.*'

As they came up the aisles after me, José's voice in English: 'Señor Connaught? Where are you? I think you should speak with us.'

The younger man reached the locked door without seeing me and then as he turned he and José, who had come up on the daïs behind him, saw me at the same time.

'Mr Connaught, what are you doing there? Perhaps you are not well?'

I put my face in my hands, rubbed hard, and looked up. José's customarily kind expression was accompanied by a quizzical sort of smile: no threat, no guns.

'I think I'm all right.'

He stepped over and helped me up.

'Are you quite sure? You look pale. Perhaps you fainted?'

'*Está en copas,*' suggested his companion, wrinkling his nose and showing not more than average perspicacity – the word *copa* is used for a measure of spirits, particularly coñac.

José shrugged. 'Nevertheless, it is very fortunate we have met you, Mr Connaught. Indeed almost a miracle since we have only just made a decision to try to find you.' He took me down into the auditorium and put me on the end of a bench – he sat on the one in front, turned with his arms on my table. His companion remained standing in the aisle.

'We have had four men watching you, your friend Maurice, and of course Paco Blas, since your arrival in Santiago,' he continued. 'But tailing – is that the right word? – is difficult with so few people in such crowds and our men are not professionals, while Blas undoubtedly is. And so we stopped following you and Maurice, and concentrated all our resources on Blas. But,' he shrugged, 'he is a professional and we lost him. We want to know if you have any idea where he might be. In fact we should like to question you very closely for any hint he may have let drop as to his intentions.'

'I don't know where he is. I'm looking for him, too.'

'Why?'

'Because Maurice might be near him, might be in danger. I have lost Maurice.'

'What brought you here looking for Maurice?'

This question was asked more sharply. I sighed, rubbed my face again. Now I was once more in personal contact with the man I found it impossible to believe he was up to no good. With him there, one knew he was a thoroughly nice person. Anxiety, fear and too much to drink had confused my perception of this.

'I thought – think – Paco Blas is trying to kill a Basque here called Rafael Llodio; and that Maurice is trying to stop him. I think this Llodio might be here in the Faculty for the . . .

'*Dios*, this must be very clever of you, for surely it is not something Blas has told you,' José was excited now and turned to his companion, speaking quickly in Spanish. Then back to me: 'This is what we have thought also – why we have been watching for a long time . . .'

'Since Nájera.'

'Ah. You recognised me there. I was not sure. Yes. Since then. Mr Connaught, would you come with us? Surely you can help us, and we might be able to help you to find Maurice also.'

193

CHAPTER 26

They took me out into the cloister, along to the next corner and up a wide flight of shallow stairs with sculptured balustrades – at the top a wide well-lit corridor. José knocked on the third door, was challenged from inside, gave a pass-word and we were let in.

The room was like a company boardroom and I assume was normally used for similar purposes – possibly for faculty meetings, that sort of thing. There was a long oval table capable of sitting perhaps thirty people, with leather-mounted blotters, good comfortable chairs, glasses, water carafes, and so on. The windows were tall, heavily curtained in brown velvet, and the drapes were closed. It was dimly lit by two chandeliers of modern design, and filled with tobacco smoke to pollution level.

There were ten people there. They looked like not too prosperous business men – not too prospersous because they were pale, looked chronically anxious, ulcer-prone. Since in their spare time they were trying to form a Basque separatist movement backed by Basque business and illegal but non-marxist trade unions, the general air of being worn down was not surprising. One man, rather older than the rest, was obviously the leader and therefore presumably Rafael Llodio. He was nearly bald, sat looking in front of him through gold-rimmed spectacles from under hooded eyelids. There were always two or three people behind him, at his sides, always he seemed to be not only the centre of focus but also something they were looking after, protecting. They must have learned to live with the idea that thugs like Paco Blas might come leaping through the door or windows spraying the landscape with bullets.

Once José had explained who I was, there was a brisk, clipped exchange between him and another man who looked more military than the others, with Señor Llodio putting in an occasional word. The rest watched and listened. They referred back to me frequently with José as interpreter and from this I was able to piece together what had happened, what was happening.

They knew of Paco Blas as a professional gunman, son of a New York Puerto Rican father and Irish mother. He had worked for the IRA and at the time of the closest cooperation between the IRA and ETA in 1973-74 was known to have worked for the ETA as well. But he was not political: simply a psychopath who made a good living at work he found congenial.

For some months Llodio's party had feared the ETA would assassinate their leader. When we told José in Ondárroa that we had helped Blas over the Pyrenees into Spain they thought the attempt was about to be made. They traced Blas to Nájera and my van a day or two after hearing reports of an unpublicised shooting incident there and from then on they had kept an eye on us and Blas. When we picked up Blas at León and I confirmed that we were due to arrive in Santiago at exactly the same time as Llodio, it seemed their suspicions had been justified.

In Santiago they had followed us, but lost Paco Blas between eleven and twelve. At a quarter-past one the man they had watching the van saw Blas return and let himself in. At two Maurice returned and almost immediately left again. Then I arrived and failed to get in and suddenly they realised the van must be empty, that somehow Blas had got out without them seeing him – here I suggested that he had changed into the green overall. They checked and found that indeed he had gone.

They reported back to Llodio at the University and Llodio refused to move. There seemed to be no point in

195

going out into the crowded streets knowing a gunman was out there waiting for him. They had just decided that it might be useful to look for Maurice and me as well as Blas when seemingly providentially I had walked straight into the Faculty just as José, the only one of them who could speak English, was leaving to find me.

They questioned me for at least half an hour trying to get some hint out of me of Blas's intentions. My drunkenness began to tail off into the beginning of hangover, I developed a foul headache – partly the tobacco smoke – and I felt sick. But my brain began to function more intelligently.

At last Rafael Llodio stretched out, tapped ash off the small cigar he was smoking and spoke – not in Spanish, it must have been Basque. The military-looking man who, through José, had been doing most of the questioning, shrugged and agreed. José translated.

'They think you cannot help further by verbal means only. Señor Llodio asks if you would go with us to your van. You have no keys. One of us would break in. With you there as owner this will be all right. You understand? There may be something in the van which you have missed that will be a clue.'

I agreed. I assumed that the damage would not be much – José assured me that they would pay to put it right. It seemed the only unexplored way of tracking down Blas, and therefore Maurice.

Out in the quadrangle again the fresh air – balmy with afternoon warmth – was like a ministering angel's caress. However, as soon as we got into the street – José, I and two others – we found another demonstration, like the one in Pamplona but not so large, was in progress. A hundred yards away, between us and the van, a dense mob with banners was just on the point of disintegrating. Again I heard the percussion of tear-gas grenades, saw the sudden turbulence as panic bit into the crowd, and again the break as of a dam and the flood of humanity

196

towards us. José pulled me into a shop, a bookshop, the two others stood in front of us. The bookseller pushed at us and begged us to get out: he feared the Forces of Order would make our presence an excuse to burst in and smash up his shop.

We saw a young man at the end of the fugitives turn, just in front of us, with a goodish camera – an SLR anyway – but he wasn't quick enough. A visored policeman with shield and truncheon swung accurately and the camera flew away into the gutter – even in the air it shed glass. A second policeman smashed it with his boot, then stooped, pulled out the cartridge and quickly shredded out the film, exposing it.

José looked at his watch: 'Four thirty. The Kings are due to arrive at five. These were our Galician separatist brothers. They planned to demonstrate to Juan Carlos but, as you see, it has been forbidden.'

The streets were now littered with torn-up pamphlets, the wretched remains of a banner, and the air was corrosive with gas. With handkerchiefs dampened at a fountain over our faces we hurried on to where the van was. I feared it might have been damaged already – it looked as if the little square by the market must have been one of the centres of the disturbance.

It turned out to be worse than that. The van was not there at all; it had gone.

'Can Maurice drive?' José asked.

'No.'

'Would he give his keys up to someone else who could, a friend, if he thought it necessary?'

I shrugged.

'I understand. He might do so, but it seems unlikely. It is more likely that Blas, or a friend of Blas, has taken it. Perhaps as a getaway car.'

'Yes.'

'We had better try to think things over again.' He

spoke in Basque to his friends. One was to stay there, watch in case the van, Maurice or Blas returned; the other was to report back to the Faculty.

José and I went to the nearest bar – the one I had tried to sober up in nearly two hours before, when I had first found the van locked and no sign of Maurice.

This time my brain was working at something nearer what I hope is its normal level of intelligence; though the headache remained like a minor migraine.

'There's one aspect of all this that bothers me,' I said while we waited for coffee again. José ordered decaffeinated. I suppose that like many of his countrymen he believes ordinary coffee makes you *nervioso*. However, I can't really believe José could ever be less than unruffled.

'It's not exactly an aspect,' I went on, conscious that I was slipping into seminar jargon, but unable to do anything about it. 'Phenotypically more an *area* that I feel I haven't properly investigated, about which I have not yet asked the right questions.'

'Go on.' No sign of nervousness at this absurd preamble, not even irritation.

'You've just asked whether or not Paco might have taken the van to use it as a getaway vehicle and, without really thinking about it, I said yes. Well, I think I was right. I mean we were. Though at first sight one would think I was wrong.'

'I am not yet understanding you.'

'Hang on. The point about getaway vehicles is this, isn't it? Whether it's to get away from an assassination or a bank robbery, there are always two. The first is driven only a short way to a rendezvous where the second is waiting, because the first will almost certainly be identified by passers-by and so on, it will be remembered by people who were at the scene of the crime . . .'

'So. If your van is to be used as a getaway vehicle, you mean it will be the second one.'

'No. Let me finish. It seems to me that Paco has been at

198

great pains to make us believe he is part of the ETA. Not only has he not denied it, he's gone out of his way to tell us that he is.'

'And therefore, whoever he is working for, it is not the ETA?'

'Exactly. But there would be no point in making Maurice and me think he is, unless, after the killing, the police come very quickly to us. And that's exactly what they will do as soon as they identify the first getaway car as an English van and so on. That is if we haven't already gone to them to report it stolen. Actually Maurice this morning began to guess that Paco had nothing to do with the ETA . . .'

'How, why did he do that?'

I explained Maurice's reasoning, based on the fact that Paco had not mentioned a particular ETA faction.

'That was clever of him,' José acknowledged, picking at his left thumb-nail with the right forefinger. 'So. Paco Blas's employer is not only an enemy of Rafael Llodio. He, or they, are enemies of the ETA as well. It must help us to know that.'

'I wish I could see why.'

'All knowledge is useful; it is only necessary to know how to use it. Let us go over the things that have not yet been explained.' He ticked them off on his fingers: 'The overall, green you said? It is unlikely that it was simply a disguise to enable him to shake off our men. He was quite able to do that without an overall. The mysterious object in a cardboard box that came with the overall. A pass-card. To what or where? Then there is the crashing of the car that belonged to your French friend . . .'

'Yes. That too bears out what I have been saying. The friend, Auguste, once told me that he knew Blas was not a . . .'

José's brow did now narrow in irritation, but not at my interruption. The bartender had flicked on a large colour television on a shelf above the counter. He beamed round at us and at the ten or twelve other customers who had come in after us, and made a complacent announcement to us all, over the martial music that was already blaring out.

'He says we will have a better view here,' José translated, 'even though we are only three hundred metres away.'

Mesmerised by the newly turned-on TV set, even though it was an unwanted intrusion, we waited for the picture to settle into focus. The canned music faded into a live babble of thousands of excited people with a commentator's voice over. I recognised, everyone recognised because a subdued 'aaaah' went round the bar as it always does when *our* town appears on telly, we recognised the interlocking flights of steps up to the façade of the Cathedral with the Moorish style *fachada* for the fireworks at the top. The camera closed in on the commentator who was standing beneath it.

'He is saying *Los Reyes,* the Kings, will come in three or four minutes. They have just left with the *infantes,* the airport. There is a motorcade.' He watched for a moment then, republican as he no doubt was, he put together an expression of boredom. But before he could return to our discussion the camera settled briefly on the RTVE vans I had seen in the morning. The technicians, as I have said, were in green overalls.

We both reacted. José went pale and his hand fastened on my wrist so that for a moment I thought he was holding me there.

'If this is it, there is nothing we can do,' he muttered. 'It's too late now, too far off.'

Monique's strange sentence 'Julius Caesar is JC is Juan Carlos' repeated itself over and over in my head, pulsing with the migraine above my eyes.

The camera closed up on the beautiful doorway of the hotel. The hall behind it, visible through glass, was filled with uniforms and vestments – gold braid, white plumes, monseigneurial reds. Then the picture opened back out over the crowd – about five thousand I should guess and increasing every second, in gay mood as far as I could see, chanting 'Juan Carlos, Juan Carlos, Sof-ee-a, Sof-ee-a.' Balloons bobbed. Children were hoisted on shoulders, there was a sudden surge forward against the barrier of police who had kept open a pathway the width of a large car from the corner of the square to the hotel entrance; and then here they came: black, closed cars, pennants fluttering, cruising like water over oiled silk, their tops only just visible above the heads of the crowd and the police; they slid smoothly to a halt. Doors opened, white gloved hands came smartly up to a salute, and as the King and Queen emerged a tight cluster of uniformed bodies congealed about them. One could just distinguish the tight bronze waves that had become so familiar from every shop window, the honey-coloured hair beneath a fine black *mantilla*. The knot of dignitaries moved swiftly across the forecourt of the hotel and on to the single step in the magnificent doorway.

For a carefully planned second the protective shield of human flesh opened out: two arms, one grey-suited the other white beneath the black lace shawl, were raised in friendly salute, then the bodyguard engulfed them again, and they were gone, into the hotel.

No shots rang out.

CHAPTER 27

With a smile which no doubt expressed relief as much as self-mockery Rafael Llodio declared: 'Well, it seems I am not as important yet as we thought. There is no point in any assassin who wants to do away with me dressing up as a television technician since I am most unlikely to appear on state television. Who would want to see me?' He lit a thin cigar, looked at its glowing end, puffed out a heavy cloud of white smoke. He was demonstrating, I thought, the qualities which had brought him to where he was: humour of an overtly self-deprecating sort, courage tempered with caution, and, that *sine qua non* of the successful politician, the habit of spelling things out slowly and carefully as if addressing an audience of ten-year-olds with the right to vote.

'Clearly Blas,' he went on, 'is working for people who hate the ETA. Clearly he is planning to assassinate someone. It need not be the King, but it might be. If it is, then he is working for the Ultras, the extreme Right. They are the only people at this moment who would gain: with the King dead, apparently shot by Marxist separatists, an extreme right-wing junta, a regency for the *Infante*, would not only be inevitable; for a time it would be widely popular. And this is the moment: the Suárez government have promised a wider amnesty which the King will announce next week; general elections; a constitution. Who knows, they may even plan to bring the Guardia Civil within the rule of law. Many Ultras, many of the *búnker* must be feeling very, very threatened. As I say, we cannot be certain, but I think we should act as if we are; act as if we *know* Blas intends to kill the King. We must try to stop him.'

He looked around as if to see if his aides approved.

'If we succeed we can expect Juan Carlos to be grateful,' he added, and the smile returned. 'It is always pleasant when expediency and right go hand in hand.

'But it isn't going to be easy,' he went on. 'Clearly there are powerful people behind Blas. Where are they? In the Guardia Civil? In the Army? In the Church? Not every Prince of the Church is as liberal as the Archbishop of Madrid. We may certainly assume that someone high up in RTVE is in the plot. And so, we may very well find our efforts obstructed at quite high levels – perhaps the highest. However, we have time: it is now six o'clock. There are to be no further television transmissions from Santiago until ten o'clock tomorrow morning when the King will go in procession to the Cathedral to hear the Mass for St James and to give his message to the nation: we must suppose that if Blas has cover as a television technician and the King is his target, that the attempt will be made then. So we have time to go carefully. If we find resistance from the Guardia Civil, a reluctance to listen to us, we can withdraw, and try the Civil Governor, and so on . . .' Thus said Rafael Llodio as far as I could gather from José's whispered translation.

They asked me to remain with them, insisting that they would need my evidence to convince the authorities that they really did have grounds for believing that an attempt on the King was planned for the next morning. Naturally I agreed though my fears for Maurice's safety were growing more acute every moment and I felt no one now was thinking about him. For half an hour I sat there, suffering my headache, almost sick with the smoke, while Llodio set into motion his plan for discreetly alerting whatever authorities might listen sympathetically. People came and went; interminable, cautiously phrased telephone conversations took place.

I began to piece together something of what Maurice must have begun to realise hours, days, even weeks ahead of me. How far I got then I can't be sure – there has been so much talk, so much questioning by the police, so much solitary speculation in this hotel room since, that I can't be sure that some of it didn't come to me later: but I do remember that I worked out then why the gunfight at Nájera had been a hoax – Paco had been firing blanks simply to convince me that he was an ETA gunman. Clearly Maurice had worked that out too, and almost straightaway; possibly even before the event took place. At any rate, and this I didn't know till later, his suspicions must have been confirmed when he found the Doctor Gómez Paco had sent him for was the Guardia Civil surgeon and not just a private practitioner.

Nor of course did I know that Maurice had received his instructions to reach Nájera when we did, not from José as I had supposed, but through the cripple in the Pamplona bull-fight queue; later they were confirmed in detail by the smooth character in the Renault 12 who parked by us during lunch the day we left Pamplona. In short, Maurice had known for a long time that Paco was in the pay of the right-wing Ultras, not the ETA. (It is unthinkable that the ETA could infiltrate the Guardia Civil – the Warriors of Christ the King, however, almost certainly have.) Paco must have guessed Maurice knew but relied on his blackmail to keep him quiet. I, an English university lecturer and therefore presumably reliable and unbiased, was to be the one to swear in good faith after the assassination that I knew Paco to be a member of the ETA.

Inklings of all these things and more I worked out in that half-hour: the substance came later. But what did come through to me with increasing certainty and searing fear with it, was that Maurice had realised, perhaps at the moment Monique had seen the fortuitous link between Julius Caesar and Juan Carlos, that Paco was planning to shoot the King, and that the silly, stupid boy had gone off on his own to try to stop him.

Why? 'None of it's anything to do with us' he had said; and one Basque killing another, or a right-wing terrorist killing a left-wing terrorist did indeed have nothing at all to do with Maurice. But with his deep and irrational attachment to the idea of royalty and to the particular persons of Juan Carlos and Sofía, regicide was another matter. It's no use thinking such attitudes are puerile or politically immature – a lot of people have them. To say, as I have, that Maurice is, was, apolitical is finally wrong: he was, is, a raving monarchist.

At about seven o'clock nothing much seemed to have happened, nothing much seemed to have been done. In considerable agony of mind, and with the resolution already half-formed that I would run for it, get back into the town and try to find Maurice, I told José that the smoke and my head were too much for me, that I was going down into the quadrangle for fresh air.

Even so I might have gone back after taking a couple of turns round the arcades: out in the open the chances of my actually finding him, of getting him out of danger seemed remote; while upstairs however slowly and cautiously, something was being done, and in a way in which I could probably assist.

But a five-year-old voice said: 'Hi!'

I looked down at the straight blonde hair, the freckles, the grubby face, the same dusty skirt trailing over flip-flops.

'Hi,' I said.

'We knowed you too in the bullfight town, didn't we?' Then she called. 'Hey, Mom. Here's the other man from the bullfight town.'

And around the corner came her identical mother and putative father.

'Why hullo there. Say, you wouldn't be looking for your friend again, would you? The guy you were looking for in Pamplona?'

205

My heart leapt.

'Actually, yes.'

'Well, this time we have seen him. Half an hour ago, eh Mary-Lou? In that big square back of the Cathedral, you know the one? The one with all those steps and like an open-air theatre.'

Then, 'Glad to be of help,' he called out after me.

CHAPTER 28

I spent the next two hours in and around the Cathedral, frantically covering the same ground again and again, frantically trying to search out corners I had overlooked. I saw no sign of Maurice, nor of Blas. The evening came on, the crowds grew, a feeling of anticipation, jolly yet solemn in the Cathedral, rather wilder, more excited outside it, began to stir through everything like a breeze, or heat coming through a cooking pot. In the big plaza between the Town Hall and the baroque façade more and more fireworks were being set up – clearly the Moorish *fachada* was to be only a part of the show; the southern side of the square was roped off and the enclosure filled with poles festooned with pale grey cylinders, strings of sausage-like packets, and batteries, rank upon rank, of rockets: to the English eye used to small pieces wrapped in gaily decorated paper they looked both oddly dull and excitingly large.

During my first couple of circuits the TV men were still busy: in green overalls, with dark wiry hair, they all looked like Blas from a distance – three or four times I edged closer with an electric taste of fear on my tongue only to find the resemblance was entirely superficial. They were setting up lights and cameras for the morning's transmission from the Cathedral, the transmission during which, if Llodio and his friends had calculated right, Blas was planning to make his attempt. Looking over the rich splendour of it all, imagining the King surrounded by prelates, generals, admirals, and paying homage at the holiest shrine in his kingdom, one could see the logic: the reaction against the supposed murderers would be almost complete and irreversible for decades.

The centre of the technicians' activity was the west end, round and above the Pórtico de la Gloria. The Pórtico is set between two large square towers, which support the baroque spires heaped up on them. Originally the porch jutted out from the mediaeval west wall which is pierced, above the porch, by four lancet windows and one rose window, all filled with plain glass; the baroque façade stands outside the Pórtico a yard or two even further west and acts as a screen to the original fabric, rising right up to and beyond the height of the mediaeval west wall. This screen also carries clear leaded glass – but the lights are far bigger than the mediaeval ones. As I noted earlier their purpose at the lower levels is to allow daylight to fall on the principal figures of the Pórtico; higher up they light the mediaeval glass.

There is therefore a narrow, high-ceilinged space above the Pórtico with the roof of the Pórtico as its floor, set between the baroque screen and the mediaeval west wall; its long sides are enclosed mainly by glass, its ends by the towers. One way it faces out over the plaza with the Town Hall, the Royal Hotel and, on that day, the fireworks beneath; the other side faces back into the Cathedral. It could hardly be bettered as a place for an outside broadcast producer faced with presenting the procession of the King, Queen, and so on, across the plaza, up the interlocking zig-zag of steps below, through the Pórtico and up the nave to the high altar. Except for the moment or two when the procession passes through the Pórtico beneath him, he can see the whole thing without relying on his monitors, and therefore can time exactly the deployment of his cameras.

Somehow, I suppose by sheer brute force, the technicians had already manhandled a console of monitors and a sound-deck up the wide stairs of the north tower and into this space. As I watched from the nave, shadowy figures silhouetted by the evening sun moved across from one lancet window to the next, presumably putting

208

the finishing touches to their preparation. In front and to the side of them, opposite the big door into the north tower which they were using, a pillar of scaffolding had been erected whose top came to the bottom ledge of the windows. There was a hooded camera already set on this structure and a battery of lights as well.

By nine o'clock when, despairing, I came through for the third time, the work was finished – the doors to the tower were closed, the cables discreetly strung together and laid up against walls or with carpeted ramps set over them, the sawdust and chippings from the odd bits of carpentry that had been necessary swept away, the spare scaffolding carried off. There was not a green overall in sight – and presumably would not be until when? say nine o'clock in the morning, an hour before the transmission was due to start. With dusk deepening I decided, without much hope of achieving anything, to widen my search beyond the immediate precincts of the Cathedral; I calculated that with the technicians gone it was unlikely that Blas would appear now.

I dragged myself round the town for an hour or so. The sky, which had been hazy, almost cloudy all day, darkened save for a luminescent glow above the Town Hall to the west which silhouetted the grandiose Bernini-style statue of St James on the roof. Street lights came on, prisms glittered beneath raftered ceilings in upstairs rooms, the principal buildings were floodlit and from almost every point in the town the twin spires of the Cathedral could be seen, encrusted obelisks glowing goldenly against the purple of the sky. The crowds were more dense, more animated; from ten o'clock onwards wherever one was there was a steady flow which I resisted, towards the big plaza. Partly to avoid this, partly because I had already covered the more important streets and squares more times than I care to remember, I took to the back streets -- the narrow cobbled alleys that link the thoroughfares or run like deep canyons between palaces and hospices. And in one of these, a lengthy almost straight street running between houses on one side and the west wall of the giant monastery of St Martin on the other, I saw the arrival, the return of my van.

I was at the end furthest from the Cathedral, walking back towards it on a narrow pavement not more than three feet wide. The street was one way and almost deserted: the far end had been closed off and access apparently limited to those who live in it; there were temporary no parking signs all along it. My van cruised past me, went on almost to the far end, did a three-point turn. I thought for a moment that it was simply going to return the way it had come, disappear again. Momentarily I wondered how I could stop it. But while it was still a clear fifty yards away, the onside wheels pulled up on to the pavement in front of me and it came to a standstill half on, half off the road, facing the wrong way up the street from the plaza and the Cathedral. The headlights died, then the sidelights. No one got out.

With my heart beating unpleasantly fast, I pulled myself into a shallowly recessed doorway and did my best to think coherently. After two minutes I gave up – no course of action could be rationally arrived at until I knew who was in the driving seat. Feeling frightened but not really sure why, I resumed my way down the street at as even a pace as I could manage, walked out in the road since my van was blocking the pavement, and managed, without a too obvious hesitation in my stride to get a clear view of the man behind the steering wheel. There was no doubt at all in my mind as to who it was – I saw him clearly in profile as I had seen him before. It was the flash young man with the Renault 12 who had pulled in to our layby between Pamplona and Logroño, who had had a girl with him then, who had carried a pistol beneath his dashboard. At that moment I did not know that he had told Maurice where and when we were to pick up Blas in Nájera, but the coincidence of his presence in Santiago, driving my van, was enough to make me sure that he was involved with Blas.

I was stunned by the implications; as soon as I was well clear of the van I broke into a short run that carried me into the small square in front of the monastery of St Martin and there collapsed on to a low granite wall.

My van was to be the first getaway vehicle, the one which would lead me to identify Blas as a member of the ETA – so much José and I had worked out correctly. But it was the timing that we had got wrong, deceived by Blas's green overall into thinking that the attempt was planned to take place during a television transmission: for here was the van, parked not more than two hundred yards, less as the crow flies, from the Hotel de los Reyes Católicos where the King was staying, and yet there were a clear twelve hours before the next broadcast. And at the wheel a second gunman, already waiting: for what? for the sound of shots, not too distant, before turning the lights on again, setting the engine running.

What was to be done? What could I do? I looked up wildly at the steady stream of people flooding past me to the big plaza to the right; I realised I was attracting puzzled or amused glances again, but no one bothered to pause – the fireworks were almost due. I buried my face in my palms, then clenched my fists and banged my forehead – what could I do?

A hand tugged my shoulder.

'Archie? Mr Connaught? Are you well?'

I looked up into Monique's face – Lili's behind her shoulder, both a little serious, concerned.

'Yes, I am. I think I am.'

'Are you sure? Can we get you something?'

'No, I'm sure. I don't need anything.'

Without quite knowing why I began to walk with them, between them, down towards the big square – it must have been their own urgency, their own desire to get there before the fireworks started that carried the

211

three of us back into the crowd: they wanted to be sure I was all right, but having done that they wanted to be sure, they said, that they had a place from where they could see both the Town Hall balcony and the *fachada* opposite without too much difficulty. Before I could make sense of this Lili went on to ask me, in her accented English: 'And where is Maurice? Why are we not having Maurice also?'

She gave his name French pronunciation, as she always did.

We were late, and before I could answer the floodlights on the spires died leaving them silhouetted black now against the night sky, and as they did the first rocket soared above the roofs, cracked, and spilled its shower of white stars over the square beneath.

The flow of the crowd slowed, thickened as we got nearer – the square must already have been nearly full. The first set piece went up, a huge cluster of rockets sun-bursting into red and gold, silver and electric blue – the colours of Spain and of Galicia – so bright they lit the upturned faces around us, and we pushed on, entering the square just as a wave of clapping flooded over the crowd towards us from the Town Hall opposite. At first I thought it was for the fireworks, but a moment later the real reason became clear, even at that distance. The long balcony, already draped with a huge hanging bearing the royal arms quartering Castilla, León, Aragón and Navarra, was slowly filling up towards its extremities as people continued to come out on to it behind the central figures who had arrived first. In front were three children, a boy and two girls, the boy about seven the girls older; behind them their mother – honey-coloured hair piled high on her head; around them uniforms, frock-coats, soutanes.

Another battery of rockets soared upwards – this time they exploded more thunderously, like cannon rather than musketry, stunning the ears and setting reverbera-

212

tions crashing from Town Hall to Cathedral; the flares that floated down glowed brightly – we could all see how the little girl had covered her ears with her hands – then 'Juan Car-los, Juan Car-los, Juan Car-los' the crowd chanted, for as the darkness rushed back the tall figure, unmistakably familiar from the new stamps and coins, joined his family on the balcony.

I knew then why Paco Blas was disguised as a television technician and I turned, elbowing, pushing, barging, fighting almost as if I was drowning, to get out of the crowd and back to the Cathedral.

The Puerta Santa, the Holy Door, which I had passed that morning, is opened at midnight on 31st December of each Holy Year, and remains open for the whole year. For twelve months the Cathedral is never closed. It was about the furthest point in the Cathedral from where I started in the Square and it took me five minutes at least to get to it.

There were lights round the altar and banks of newly lit candles guttering as I half-walked, half-ran past them, but the main body of the great nave was in darkness, the chandeliers extinguished, yet again and again, even as I rushed towards the west end, the great columns and the huge vault were lit up with hectic flickering light thrown through the outer layers of glass and then through the four lancet windows and the rose above the Pórtico de la Gloria as the fireworks continued outside; and the air inside was bruised by the percussions and explosions.

There were few if any people about, I noticed none: the racket outside would have been a bar to devotion for all but the blind or deaf. When I got to it the great door to the north tower was locked, of course. For a moment or two I could only lean against it gasping for breath, and fighting the despair that threatened to flood me: how could I possibly get that door open? How could I find anyone who would listen to me, understand me?

Then more light, green this time, lit up the kneeling

213

figure of Maestro Mateo in front of me and the scaffolding beyond hung with unlit lamps like sightless eyes reflecting the rockets, and on the top the weird hooded presence of a TV camera. There was a metal ladder.

I hauled myself up it, the rungs cold to my hands, flung myself across the tiny platform and then my breath caught in horror as the whole structure swayed and for a second I thought I was to be plunged thirty feet down to the stone flags below – but no doubt it was properly stable, more stable than it felt.

My feet were now on a level with the bottom ledge of the extreme left-hand lancet window and about eight feet away from it. By leaning over the rail I could see about one third of the space above the Pórtico. Not much, but enough to make out in the garish uneven light a console of monitors, heaps of cable – and the figure of Blas sprawled out on his stomach. He had removed a leaded pane of glass from the bottom row in the outer window and was watching the distant balcony across the square through binoculars. He was about twenty feet from me with the glass of the inner window between us.

The light died, then came again shifting eerily to red as the sky outside bled fire.

There was no sign of Maurice – and it was, as it had been since he disappeared, Maurice who mattered to me. I waited, indecisively, to see what would happen next. Blas put down the binoculars, peered at the watch on his wrist, shielding it against the light so he could see the luminous numerals.

Down in the plaza, eight giant catherine wheels began to spin and the light they shed settled for perhaps a minute and a half into a steady glow – by it I could just make out the tall figure, the bronze hair, only the head really visible above and between two smaller men who stood protectively in front of him.

Blas moved and I saw the kit-bag lying beside him. He pulled out the parts of his rifle and began to assemble

214

them. He worked briskly, doing something he had done too often before and he hardly took his eyes off the balcony. He slotted in a magazine and then, with more care, a telescopic sight lifted from the tissue wrapping in the box I had seen in the van. This clipped over the rear sight of the rifle.

As the wheels fizzled out (I think now their ignition might have been some sort of cue for the killer: what followed indicates that he knew the final sequence of the show), he wriggled a little, settled himself, put his eye to the sight (infra-red?), and as he did I began to scream: what, I don't know – I suppose it was in English.

Above the noise of the fireworks Blas heard me, turned his head, looked full in my direction but probably could not see me – from where he was the light must have reflected back at him off the glass between us. Then he turned back and raised the sight to his eye again.

Outside a large rocket failed and I must assume it had been tampered with. It rose only to the height of the college roof and exploded there filling the whole square with a light more intense and a crash more deafening than any before, and Blas fired.

He fired again and again, three single shots then, as the puppet figure far away across the square continued to watch the fireworks as if magically protected, Blas began to fumble and tear manically at the useless magazine of blanks, desperately trying to replace it, but before he could the final act of the display – which would have provided the cover he needed for a successful getaway – began.

The hundreds of flares set in the *fachada* below us ignited simultaneously and immediately the entire complex of glass and stone we were looking through was covered by a pall of smoke, white, blue, green, red, the colours changed as the flares burnt lower, and the Square, the Town Hall, its balcony and the tall man on it were quite curtained off.

At this moment all (it seemed like all) the lights in the Cathedral came on together and the hollow nave echoed with shouts and clattering feet. Coming down towards us from the Holy Door were five or six armed police-men, other men I knew nothing of, and in the rear José Zumárraga swinging along on his rubber-shod stick.

For all this, five fatal minutes elapsed before they got the tower door open – time enough for me to get down and join them, time enough for José to explain breath-lessly that my van had been spotted, that the smooth driver had talked as soon as he realised that he would be shot out of hand if he didn't, time enough for Paco Blas to escape out on to the roofs.

CHAPTER 29

Dear Maurice, no one will know for certain what you had been doing since two o'clock and just how you managed to get on to the roof of the Cathedral, and until you are well enough and ready enough to live through the experience again, no one is going to ask you – not if I can help it. But one thing I am sure about is why you did not go to the police.

Teniente López, the Guardia with the orange mole who speaks English, asked me to speculate on this the other day and it gave me some pleasure to answer him as bluntly as I could. It's common knowledge, I told him, that the Guardia Civil and their Ultra allies are a law unto themselves: at this moment they are 'protecting' the murderers of the woman of Santurce, of the Carlists shot dead at Montejurra, and the perpetrators of countless less publicised acts of terrorism against moderates and liberals. They refuse to submit to public inquiry into the many, perhaps hundreds of incidents when uniformed Guardias have fired on and killed people – from foreign tourists to slogan writers. As Llodio hinted, the day Juan Carlos announces that he is going to clean out the Guardia Civil and force them to act within the law will be the most dangerous of his life: the fact that you, Maurice, knew that Paco had had help from at least one or two individual Guardias must have predisposed you to believe that the plot he was a part of was an attempt to pre-empt that day.

What could you have expected if you had returned to the Cuartel? At the best: 'Yes, of course there's a plot to assassinate the King, we know of at least ten and we're already doing our best to stop them – your fantasies will

217

be a drain on our manpower we can ill afford.' At the worst, and just as likely, 'Yes, of course there's a plot to kill the King, and we're in it – kindly step into this cell until it's all over.'

As I say, I enjoyed telling the Teniente all this. He made no comment; his face lost its bonhomie and went hard: I think he took the point.

I made no mention, have not mentioned to anyone, that Blas was blackmailing you.

Dear Maurice – what then did you do? I imagine you followed Blas from the van, and from his movements worked out what his intentions were, how accurately I do not know. But you must have realised he was planning to shoot the King from somewhere on the façade of the Cathedral; you must have found that his overall, his pass-card, had got him and his kit-bag to parts of the fabric you could not reach by orthodox means. You resorted to the unorthodox. In all the mélange of architecture, of baroque and rococo ornamentation, of side chapels and buttresses at the east end of the Cathedral you found a way up on to the roof of the apse – presumably you waited till dark before making this ascent.

The roof of the apse has a balustrade, there are pinnacles, obelisks. Then there is the huge domed lantern above the high altar, from the inside centre of which the giant censer is swung. Somehow you got round this – and then you stuck. In front of you stretched a simple unornamented, steeply gabled roof, the roof of the nave, nearly a hundred yards long with no holds, no supports, a hundred feet or more above the ground; you stayed where you were with your back to the columns which support the dome, unable through your vertigo to go on or go back.

I am not sure by which I am moved the more: admiration for the courage which brought you so far; pity for the terror you must have felt. I caught a sense of your vertigo on the side of the mountain on the way down, after Blas had left us: I dare not allow myself to imagine what the complete experience is like.

Blas was immune to the feeling. Realising his planned escape was cut off, he worked his way along the roof-tree of the nave quite easily, quite quickly, reached the dome where you were hidden in the shadows between two pillars with the thick smoke of the *fachada* billowing around you, and the pealing of the bells for Sant'Iago's Day crashing about you. Blas reached you before the police, with José and me behind, found their way out after him.

Perhaps you believed he had successfully killed the King. If you did, you must have been filled with bitterest remorse, disgust, at your inability to fight off your vertigo. At all events, you tried to stop Blas. There may have been a brief struggle. Together you fell, by stages, down steep roofs, over gutters, finally to the ground.

Today they have moved you to a private room and you have had a light meal. The doctor is satisfied that you are out of danger. I'm betrayed by my relief into a black joke – trust you to land with Blas beneath you. Black because he was dead on arrival.

The doctor has also told me that your physical and mental rehabilitation may be a long and tiresome business – he is not satisfied with your left leg; he had hoped that your involuntary reactions would improve more quickly.

I'll do the best I can to help you; I promise.

When I wrote the last sentence above, I did not think there would be anything to add. But there is.

After writing it, I went downstairs and watched the hotel TV in the lounge yet again. The King and Queen were leaving for La Coruña on this the ninth and last day of their Galician tour. The commentator reported that they were a little late, having paid an unscheduled visit to the hospital here in Santiago.

219

This evening I found you with that silly inane grin on your face, the one you wore when you made that ridiculous joke about a lot of Basques in one exit. On your bedside table was a silver scallop shell, like the ones they sell in the Square of Silversmiths. A present.

I do think someone might have told me that a visit was going to take place.

And finally: today I went back to the van for the first time for a week. It's now parked outside the town. I couldn't get in, really I couldn't, not for several minutes after I'd opened the door.

Lili's León cheese has committed a nuisance.